This

Walk...
saw E...
inspiration she needed as she tapped lightly on
the cold glass. Then again, harder.

He paused, detecting the sound, and looked up.

Following her instincts, she dropped the towel,
but left the sheer curtain drawn. His eyes seemed
to stare right into hers, even through the curtain.

Slowly lifting her leg, she planted her toes on
the bottom windowsill, a shiver running through
her. She reached to get some of the spicy-scented
lotion, bending forward to work it up her leg,
over her thigh.

She let her head fall back as she applied lotion
to her neck and throat, and then finally to her
breasts, lingering there.

Then the slam of a door.

Something dropped to the floor.

Heavy boot steps on the stairs.

The next thing she knew, Ely was there, standing
in the doorway of her bedroom.

His eyes were hot, watching her, hunger etched
into every contour of his face....

Dear Reader,

We have exciting news! Starting in January, the Harlequin Blaze books you know and love will be getting a brand-new look. And it's *hot!* Turn to the back of this book for a sneak peek....

But don't worry—nothing else about the Blaze books has changed. You'll still find those unforgettable love stories with intrepid heroines, hot, hunky heroes and a double dose of sizzle!

So be sure to check out our new supersexy covers. You'll find these newly packaged Blaze editions on the shelves December 18th, 2012, wherever you buy your books.

In the meantime, check out this month's red-hot reads.

LET IT SNOW by Leslie Kelly and Jennifer LaBrecque
(A Blazing Bedtime Stories Holiday Edition)

HIS FIRST NOELLE by Rhonda Nelson
(Men Out of Uniform)

ON A SNOWY CHRISTMAS NIGHT by Debbi Rawlins
(Made in Montana)

NICE & NAUGHTY by Tawny Weber

ALL I WANT FOR CHRISTMAS
by Lori Wilde, Kathleen O'Reilly and Candace Havens
(A Sizzling Yuletide Anthology)

HERS FOR THE HOLIDAYS by Samantha Hunter
(The Berringers)

Happy holidays!

Brenda Chin
Senior Editor
Harlequin Blaze

Samantha Hunter

HERS FOR THE HOLIDAYS

HARLEQUIN®
entertain, enrich, inspire™

Recycling programs
for this product may
not exist in your area.

ISBN-13: 978-0-373-79732-5

HERS FOR THE HOLIDAYS

Copyright © 2012 by Samantha Hunter

www.Harlequin.com

Printed in U.S.A.

ABOUT THE AUTHOR

Samantha Hunter lives in Syracuse, New York, where she writes full-time for Harlequin Books. When she's not plotting her next story, Sam likes to work in her garden, quilt, cook, read and spend time with her husband and their dogs. Most days you can find Sam chatting on the Harlequin Blaze boards at Harlequin.com, or you can check out what's new, enter contests or drop her a note at her website, www.samanthahunter.com.

Books by Samantha Hunter

To get the inside scoop on Harlequin Blaze and its talented writers, be sure to check out blazeauthors.com.

All backlist available in ebook. Don't miss any of our special offers. Write to us at the following address for information on our newest releases.

Harlequin Reader Service
U.S.: 3010 Walden Ave., P.O. Box 1325, Buffalo, NY 14269
Canadian: P.O. Box 609, Fort Erie, Ont. L2A 5X3

Many friends offered their support and good cheer during the writing of this book—many thanks to Selena Blake, Anne Calhoun, Donna Cummings, Cari Quinn, Serena Bell and Ruthie Knox, who all listened, read, critiqued and cheered me on. And here I thought Ely would be the easy brother.

Also thanks to Jamie DeBree for her research info on Billings, MT, and tattoos, as well as for general cheering on.

1

ELY BERRINGER walked out of the shower into the room he rented over a restaurant in Clear River, Montana. A chill worked over his damp skin, and he eyed the thickening frost on the windows. A strand of Christmas lights attached to the outside of the building fell loose and now hung down in the center of the glass, still merry as they danced in the wind.

This was a long way from Antigua, that was for sure. He'd come home thinking that his sister-in-law, Tessa, had called him about some family trouble, but her concern had been about Lydia Hamilton, her best friend. That had given Ely a moment of pause; he and Lydia had some history he wasn't sure he wanted to reopen. But he was a Marine, and he was a Berringer—helping was what he was trained to do.

Lydia had left suddenly, according to Tessa, canceling her appointments and closing her shop until further notice. She'd been acting strangely, being distant and uncommunicative. Like she was so warm and cuddly the rest of the time, Ely thought with a snort as he dried off and got dressed. The petite Goth hottie who ran the tattoo shop, Body Inc., next to Tessa's soap shop was tough as nails. Though she could be soft as a kitten in bed, something he knew from personal experience.

Lydia told Tessa she'd be gone for a while, but had not answered her phone or responded to her email since. Tessa thought she could be in some kind of trouble, and she could be right.

Ely hadn't known Lydia for long, but even he knew how she was all over the internet—she was constantly accessing her email and social media pages, and none of them showed any recent activity. She was also serious about her business. Closing up shop at one of the busiest retail times of the year was enough to trigger his concern, as well.

He got to work and used the resources available to him through Berringer Bodyguards—the family business—and through Tessa's father, a U.S. Senator. It didn't take long to track Lydia down. She'd left a trail of credit card purchases, including a rental car that she'd returned in Billings, Montana. That likely was her final destination, so now, here he was, freezing his ass off in Montana, three weeks before Christmas.

Ice and snow obscured any view out of the windows of his small room. Born in Philadelphia, he wasn't any stranger to winter, but cold seemed to take on a new meaning out here. His flights had been delayed due to several strong weather systems crossing the U.S. At least he'd landed in Billings the day before, beating the worst of the weather. The Antiguan beach he had been standing on only a few days ago seemed a million miles away now.

As soon as he'd gotten into town, he'd asked around for Lydia and found people knew her—or her family.

She wasn't just a visitor, she'd grown up here. He'd found more in the public records at the local town hall.

He was still trying to get his head around the fact that Clear River, population 1,738, was her hometown. That wouldn't be such a surprise if Lydia hadn't told all of them that she didn't have any family. Everyone thought she'd grown up in the east as a foster kid and then ran away, out on her own at seventeen.

Not according to what he'd found.

He'd looked up her birth records in the local government office. Only child, both parents gone. He found her yearbook at the local school library, and her parents' obituaries in the newspaper. Her mother, Faye, had died less than a month ago. Obviously, that had been the trigger for the unusual behavior Tessa had noticed.

For some reason, Lydia didn't want anyone knowing what she was doing here, or that her mother had died. Or that she had a family and a past at all. What could be so awful that Lydia would want to hide it from the people who were closest to her?

Her name wasn't listed with that of her graduating class, and there were no pictures in the yearbook after her sophomore year. So maybe part of her story was true, that she had run away when she was sixteen or seventeen. Was there some horrible family secret that had caused her to flee? Ely frowned. He hated thinking she might have suffered like that in her past, but in the end, it was no one's business but hers.

Ely had secrets, too, and he didn't feel right prying into Lydia's. Still, he planned to find out a little more before he left, just to make sure she really was okay. Dealing with the death of a parent was no small thing, and Ely suspected handling it all alone was not a great idea. Still, he could easily imagine Lydia running away to lick her wounds in private, not asking for help, and not wanting anyone to know.

She wasn't one for getting too close, at least, not emotionally. They'd ended up in her bed only a few hours after they'd met. A classic one-night stand, but Lydia rocked his world and made him reconsider what he wanted in life—hence his own escape to Antigua. He'd lived there, solo on a beach for several weeks, clearing his head, thinking about his priorities, until Tessa had called.

Lydia had to be here now to settle her mother's affairs. That morning, he'd waited down the road outside her family's ranch and had watched her leave. He followed her on her errands for most of the afternoon. Lawyers, real estate, some other stores and offices.

It confirmed what he'd found so far. She didn't seem to be in any trouble, and she looked fine. Better than fine, really. He'd call Tessa in the morning and let her know her friend was okay, and leave it at that. If the storms passed, he'd head home for Christmas, or maybe he'd go back to the beach. Ely had taken a new lease on life, and Lydia had been the cause of that.

He'd become more spontaneous and wanted to enjoy life more. Having spent more than a decade of his life surrendering to his sense of duty, joining the Marines when he was eighteen and doing nine years there before coming home three years ago, when he immediately took up work with his brothers. His focus for all of his adult life had been work, family, country.

But where was he in all of that? He'd never stopped to ask. He thought he knew what he wanted—work and a family of his own—to find someone, settle down, live a traditional kind of life. The things he was supposed to want, right?

But everything had been turned upside down when the woman he thought he could have that life with betrayed him and then he ended up in bed with the last woman he could imagine sleeping with. Lydia wasn't someone he would have normally been attracted to, and she had expanded his sexual horizons far past his previous experience.

And he enjoyed it.

It was enough to make a guy seriously rethink his wants, needs and desires. For now, he was living day to day and trying to be more open. Experimenting. Not tying himself down. Why on earth had he been so anxious to marry after being tied to the military, then to his job? He fought for the freedom of others, but hadn't experienced much of his own. Maybe he'd still settle down someday, but he had a lot of living to do first.

As soon as he finished this job.

He left the room and walked downstairs to get a beer and some dinner. Crossing the restaurant to find a seat at the bar, he took note of the other patrons conversing and enjoying an end-of-the-day brew.

Lydia was a city girl—polished and street-wise. If anyone had asked, he would have assumed the closest she'd ever been to a cow would have been pouring milk for her cereal in the morning. That was about as close as Ely had ever been to one, himself. Guns, he knew. Strategy, war, protection.

Cows, not so much.

Looking at the rough, hardworking men who sat at the bar, Ely took in the Christmas tree that stood in the corner, cheerfully decorated, giving a little sparkle to the soft light off the well-worn but comfortable tavern. He caught the eye of the bartender, who walked over.

"I'll have a beer, a burger and some fries, if you're still serving," he said, with a glance at the clock.

"We are. Serve til nine," the guy said. "Some of the best local beef you'll ever taste. Visit a good one so far?"

"Yeah, it's a beautiful place."

"Business in town?"

"Not really. Just passing through to see a friend, then heading back home," Ely said casually.

"Who's your friend?"

"Lydia Hamilton. You know her?"

The bartender shook his head. "Nope. I knew Faye Hamilton, everyone did, but never met Lydia. She must be the daughter?"

"Yeah."

"Heard she took off years ago, before I bought this place, and I've had it for a while. You back from the war?"

"How could you tell?"

"I served, my father served in World War II, and my son is in Iraq. Marine?"

Ely nodded.

"Ooh-rah," the older man said with a smile, and Ely shook the hand he offered. "My name's Tom. You?"

"Ely."

They talked for a while about their service, and Ely was glad for the diversion away from the topic of Lydia.

Ideally, she would never know he was here; he had a feeling she wouldn't take kindly to the knowledge. He didn't intend to tell Tessa anything other than that Lydia was fine. Lydia had a right to her privacy, and he didn't want to mess up Tessa's friendship with Lydia. If Lydia wanted to tell Tessa about her past, that was up to her.

He didn't like lying to them, but it wasn't really

lying; it was keeping Lydia's confidence. Ely had a lot of things he couldn't tell anyone after his military years.

Tessa was a new bride, and she saw romance and happily-ever-after in everything these days. He figured she'd seen that with him and Lydia as well, and he didn't want to encourage her. She'd pressed them both for details about what had happened that night, but she was bound for disappointment on that score. What had happened between Lydia and Ely hadn't had anything to do with romance.

It had been raw, basic lust. And Lydia wasn't the romantic type.

I don't do relationships, she'd told him that night as she had undressed him. *But I do a lot of other things.*

Being with Lydia had been…liberating.

Unfortunately, they'd parted on somewhat awkward terms, and he had gone out of his way to avoid contact with her so that no one—namely Tessa—got any ideas. Also because he was messed up—he'd jumped from one woman's bed to another, and had been pretty well turned around. Not his most shining hour.

They should have cleared the air sooner, agreed to be friends, at least, since there was no doubt they would see each other from time to time. Jonas was very fond of her, too, and Ely knew Lydia would be included in whatever family functions came along. He figured time would let it fade, and they'd be friends.

Ely's attention snapped to as he realized he had completely zoned out on what the bartender was saying. He covered by nodding to the weather report playing on the TV above the bar.

"Looks like a big storm coming in."

"We get a lot of those. Hope you're not in a hurry to

get out. Will be a few days before roads are clear and planes are on time again, most likely."

"I'm in no hurry," he fibbed with a smile. He'd hoped to be there no more than one more day, but the weather appeared to have something to say about that.

His dinner arrived and Ely dug into his burger—which really was excellent—and then froze midbite.

Lydia.

She stood inside the door, scanning for a place to sit. Ely turned away, hoping she didn't see him. There'd be no way to explain his presence here other than the truth, and that wasn't an option. When he looked back, she was finding her way to one of the faded orange vinyl booths that lined the far wall. She looked small and cold in a leather jacket that wouldn't protect her well enough against this kind of weather. City girl, indeed.

She sure stood out among the locals. A few men followed her progress as she walked; the way her beautiful little backside was encased in tight jeans drew more than one appreciative gaze, the sexy piercing and her half-moon tat at the corner of her lip. It made Ely remember far too much.

He remembered biting her there, and that she'd liked it.

She'd nipped him back, and he'd liked that, too.

Lydia didn't mind a little rough play and could hold her own on that score. He was suddenly, unexpectedly hard, and shifted in his seat, cursing under his breath. Obviously seeing her up close packed more of a punch than when he was following her around in the truck all day.

Damn, she was hot. He guessed they would need a lot more time to let the effects of that one night fade.

Her black hair was a little longer, flaxen, slightly

curled at the edges as it danced around her pale skin, accentuating dark eyes and full lips. He knew that her skin, under the coat and sweater, was covered in ink… something he'd never found sexy on a woman before, but when he'd been with her, he hadn't been able to get enough of looking at the sexy designs that covered most of her body. Running his hands over them, tracing them, tasting them.

Ely had one tattoo, the symbol penned on his shoulder that he shared with the guys in his squad. Other than that, there had never been anything meaningful enough to him that he would want to inscribe it permanently on his body.

He finished his food, but barely tasted anything as he peeked at her in between bites. Taking her coffee from the server with a smile, Lydia pulled a book from her bag, sitting there, alone, reading. Her apartment had been filled with books.

Ely suspected there was far more behind the ink than anyone knew. Maybe that's why she covered herself in it, as well as the piercings that accented various points on her body—lip, ear, belly button, and one even lower that had totally surprised and turned him on.

But maybe, in some way, it was her armor. A way of hiding her secrets? Who she was, why she was here, and what was in her past that she was so intent on hiding. He knew, since he had his own. It had been necessary to survive in the war, and even when he'd come home. He ordered another beer, intending to call it a night and go back to his room before she spotted him. If he was going to be stuck here for a few days, he'd have to lay low.

Then a guy sauntered up to the booth and slid in on the opposite side from Lydia. She didn't put her book down, but the cowboy didn't take the hint. He smiled, leaning back and picked up a sugar packet from the bin on the table, playing with it between his fingers, appearing casual. Ely knew his look; the guy was obviously hoping to score that evening. Lydia peered over top of her reading and said something that made the guy's smile widen.

Ely's back stiffened, his body tightening as if for a fight. She'd probably been with others since him—why not? It was none of his business.

When he saw Lydia shake her head, smiling in a forced, false way as she brushed him off, Ely's blood pressure lowered. Something primal emerged at the thought of another man's hands on her—this guy, in particular—and didn't settle until the cowboy rejoined his friends at the bar.

Ely nursed his beer and pretended to watch the news. Eventually, she closed her book, walked to the door. She wasn't wearing the heavy eyeliner or makeup that she normally did. Still, there was something dramatic and sexy about her, making it hard to look away.

As she headed out, Ely saw the guy who had been talking to Lydia walk out the door behind her. With a buddy. The hair on the back of his neck went up. Putting the rest of his beer on the counter, he followed them outside.

LYDIA HAD HAD such a frustrating day. Heading back to the house alone had seemed unappealing after spending a good part of the afternoon waiting on her mother's lawyer, who never did show up. The will was clear— she had inherited everything—but her mother mandated that for her to collect, Lydia had to stay home for a month. Obviously her mother had good intentions, always having insisted that Lydia had to face her past.

Lydia didn't agree.

She needed to sell the ranch as quickly as possible—which meant staying the month, three more weeks—and then leave for good. But the world seemed to be working against her.

The house needed some necessary repairs, and she had tried to line up someone to do them sooner than later, unsuccessfully. Then, she'd looked into tracking down the one Realtor in Clear River. They were closed on Wednesdays. Of course. Strike three. It was Christmas in a small town. This was not going to be easy.

Many of the contractors were already booked or not scheduling new work until spring. She'd gotten some suggestions for businesses in the city, but that would add to the cost considerably.

On top of that, one of the cows was sick, and they'd had to call for the vet. Necessary and costly. The animal would be fine, thank goodness…Lydia had sat with her most of the night before, taking turns with Smitty, the ranch manager. He and one ranch hand, a sour guy named Kyle Jones, were the only two hires her mother had kept on.

She might have to see if she could take a loan against the house to make repairs and ask Smitty to talk to someone about selling the livestock. She'd forgotten how much she liked the cows. Peaceful creatures, mostly. She was glad her mother had reduced their herd to this small group of gentle dairy cows, but she had to make sure they found a good home, not some meat market.

It was all so overwhelming. Lydia felt trapped, her present life held hostage to her past, and she didn't like it. She'd left her life here behind, and she wanted to keep it that way.

But if she just walked away, she would lose the property, and her chance to sell it. With money from a sale, she could expand her business back in Philadelphia, open a second location of Body Inc., which would also mean hiring a second artist. It was a dream she didn't think she could attain for several years, but sale of her family home would make it possible.

Thinking about it made her crave the city, and she took in her surroundings as icy wind whipped her hair around her face, freezing her ears and nose.

The town was still pretty and well-kept, as it always had been. Twinkling lights decorated most of the buildings and were strung from streetlight to streetlight, their cheerfulness contrasting with the storm clouds that blotted out the stars. She'd heard they were expecting the first real snow overnight.

Most of the old, low-profile, Western-style buildings were still in place here, though there were a few new constructions. Across the street she saw an architects' office and a new medical practice that looked pretty upscale for the small town. The street was repaved, the sidewalks new, with large wooden raised gardens placed intermittently along the main street. Where plants would grow in the summer, they were now covered with snow.

As a kid, she had often gone to the pizza shop down the road with her friends after football games and to the tack store with her father. Every year, she would bake dozens of cookies with her mother for the Fourth of July picnic that always accompanied fireworks at the edge of town. Clear River always had its own little holiday parades with their local bands and town officials, and all of the kids would do something creative to show off. The town itself was often more like an extended family, everyone knowing everyone else. It had been a nice way to grow up. Mostly.

She'd been the Fireworks Princess when she was thirteen—the girl with most spark—she remembered with a smile. She'd had a lot of good times here, before things had gone bad.

The same huge spruce grew in front of town hall, even bigger than it had been, and was decorated for the season. That would have been done Thanksgiving weekend, and the annual Winter Festival, a Clear River tradition, should be coming up soon, but Lydia didn't see any announcement. Had it been canceled? If so, that was unfortunate. Snowman-building contests, craft booths, hot cocoa and treats…it was always the perfect build-up to Christmas.

Ah, well. Things changed. She sure had.

Hailey's, the inn where she'd eaten, had always been a mainstay in the town, and was still mostly the same as she remembered. It was the only place in town that rented rooms, though she'd noticed some of the other ranches had taken to including tourism packages, probably to stay financially viable. Hailey's had also always been a hangout for the local cowboys, one of whom had wanted to get friendlier than she wanted tonight.

She was no stranger to one-night stands—she preferred them, in fact—but not here, not now, and certainly not with some drunk ranch worker. Apparently he'd thought, because of her look or because she was there alone, that she might want some fun. She'd set him straight and fast.

The cold crept over her body as she stood there, and she decided she'd had enough walking down memory lane. Fat snowflakes began to fall as if on cue, sticking to her face and hair as she made her way to her car. This would be the first major storm of the season.

A slight shiver of excitement worked its way down her spine. She'd always liked the first big snowstorm. Unlike summer thunderstorms—which sometimes brought nightmarish tornadoes and dangerous lightning strikes that scared the wits out of her—the winter storms were relatively peaceful and soft, snow piling up like a secret overnight.

Lost in thought, she hadn't noticed anyone following her until she heard the footsteps, a man's low chuckle. Lydia hadn't lived on the street in some time, but she recognized the tightening of her stomach, the tingle at the base of her neck that signaled danger. She'd learned not to ignore such things and picked up her step, reaching into her bag to grab her keys, holding them firmly, sharp ends pointing out. She wished she had her mace, but hadn't counted on needing it out here.

She pressed the button to open the doors of her rental, but wasn't quite fast enough; they caught up with her as she opened the door of the car, the good ol' boy from the roadhouse and a friend, slamming it shut before she could get inside.

"Hey, darlin'," said the one who had joined her in her booth earlier. "Want some company on the dark ride home?"

"Told you already, I'm not interested," she said rudely, making eye contact to let them know she wasn't afraid.

She was though, and willed someone to drive down the damned street already. It would figure that every time she left her house she bumped into someone from her past, but now, when she wished someone would appear, everyone was inside, hunkering down before the storm.

"Well, you don't know that, do you? You think you're from the city, so you're better than us? We can live pretty fast here, too," he said.

The men closed in, and panic clawed her chest. She stepped backward, wondering if she made a run for it, toward the roadhouse, how far she'd get.

"Get lost. I will press charges, and I'll make sure you don't walk away from whatever you have in mind." While she talked, she pressed the buttons on the key fob—this thing had to have some kind of car alarm she could set off.

Sure enough, as she pressed the buttons several times, the lights and horn suddenly started blaring in annoying rhythm, filling the street with sound. As the cowboy pulled back in surprise, survival adrenaline kicked in. Lydia brought her foot up, stomping the foot of the one closest to her and then kneed him in the family jewels, sending him howling to the snowy surface as she got inside of her car and locked the doors.

Gunning the engine, she noticed a few people emerging from the restaurant and a local drugstore to see what was happening, probably making sure it wasn't their own car being broken into. The cowboys got out of the way as she did a quick U-turn in the center of the road, nearly running over the foot of the guy who had threatened her. He swore loudly after her as she raced away.

As she caught her breath and reassured herself that she was safe, she glanced to the side, and nearly hit the brakes as she caught a glimpse of a face she thought she recognized.

Ely?

His hood up, face shadowed, the man who sat in the

dark cab of a truck looked like him, but…that wasn't possible.

She watched as the truck lit up in her rearview and pulled away in the opposite direction, making her shake her head as she slowed down and got hold of herself. Great, now she was imagining things.

Her slamming heartbeat finally calmed as she drove, and she shook off the remnants of panic from the confrontation. She was fine. She had handled things herself, as she always did. If Lydia knew anything, it was how to take care of herself. She'd been doing it ever since she left home.

A momentary spark of worry had her checking her rearview for headlights, worried the cowboys might take after her—those guys wouldn't enjoy being bested by a girl—but nothing was there. Most likely, they would go home, pass out and hope their wives or girlfriends didn't get word of their bad behavior. There was nothing to worry about, she reassured herself.

Snowflakes picked up more density on the windshield, and she didn't really relax until she made it back to the ranch. Smitty and Kyle were in the bunkhouses, if she needed them, anyway.

Ely's face flashed again in her mind as she parked the car in the garage and sat there for a moment, thinking. The guy in the truck couldn't possibly have been him, though she had felt the same keen sense of awareness she had felt the first moment she had ever seen him, in a hospital emergency room. She'd been there with Tessa, when Jonas's vision had returned. She and Ely had gone for a cup of coffee. After that, they went to her place.

It was only one night, but she'd replayed it in her head about a thousand times, much to her annoyance.

Lydia had made sure he knew the rules—she didn't

do relationships. At the time, he'd just ended something bad with another woman, but he was cute and she took him home. That was all there was to it. Lydia preferred not to get too wrapped up in details—they made everything messy and complicated. Sex was fun, and she liked to keep it that way.

But she hadn't ever felt a connection—physical and otherwise—with anyone like she had with Ely. It had rattled her hard enough to send her running in the other direction, and fast. He had, too.

As it turned out, though, he had probably regretted their night together more than she imagined. That had hurt a bit. She had remained friends with a couple of the guys she'd slept with, and Ely's clear desire to have nothing to do with her after their night together had been, well, hurtful. It was like he was ashamed of being with her, which she supposed he might have been. She knew that she wasn't his usual type; he was more into classy, professional, *coiffed* chicks.

Yes, she had looked up his ex on the internet. Sadly. Suffice it to say they didn't run in the same circles at all.

She shook it off. Being here was making her moody. Dealing with losing her mother, her past, and all the complications of her inheritance were bad enough, and the holidays always messed with people's heads. It was why she normally left and went to a beach somewhere over Christmas and ignored it all.

But the nagging feeling that something was lacking in her life wouldn't quite go away. Being in Tessa's wedding, and seeing how happy she and Jonas were, didn't help matters any. It made Lydia think maybe she could find the same kind of real connection with someone, something that would last.

Crazy. She'd always enjoyed her freedom and her

work had become her life. She'd never wanted anything else. She was happy as she was. If it wasn't broken, don't fix it. She had more than she ever imagined having, and needed to be content with that.

But even if she did ever find something permanent, it wouldn't be with Ely Berringer, so she had to get him out of her head.

Easier said than done, apparently.

2

ELY LEFT HIS TRUCK about a hundred feet back on the road that led to Lydia's ranch and walked the rest of the way toward the house so as not to be spotted. He'd followed her to make sure no one else did—namely, the guys who had cornered her by her car. He'd intended to step in, but she'd taken care of things pretty well on her own.

Lydia was one tough cookie, no doubt about it, he thought with a spark of admiration. Even so, Ely wanted to pound the guy who had tried to mess with her. He settled for calling in an anonymous tip to the local authorities before he drove away.

As she'd passed him on the road, he'd made the mistake of looking toward her car. For a split second, their eyes met—she'd seen him. He thought his goose was cooked, but she'd continued to drive and was clearly too panicked to have registered that it was him. His hood had been up, face obscured by the snow and the dark.

But it had been a close call.

He made his way to the edge of the trees in time to watch her pull her car into the detached garage. What was she doing? She sat for a while before she got out and walked around to the door of the huge ranch house. His hoodie wasn't exactly the right gear for this kind of surveillance, but he hadn't expected to be out in the woods that evening when he'd headed down for supper. He put it out of his mind, ignored the cold. Not important. He'd make sure she was safely tucked in, then he'd go back.

The area was very remote, rural. The next ranch was at least five miles away. An animal sound—a horse—came from one of the barns, breaking the temporary silence, and Ely shook his head.

None of it seemed like the Lydia he knew.

Then again, no one seemed to know her. Not really. Least of all him.

Unlike the cheerfulness of the town, the ranch was cold and dark except for some lights in a few of the outbuildings away from the house. No Christmas lights or such hung here. That was okay—it made it easier for him to move around undetected.

After she went inside, he watched the lights in the windows as she turned them on, moving through the house. The next thing he knew, he saw her slim form behind the shimmer of curtains upstairs.

Undressing.

He followed the movement of her silhouetted form as she lifted her sweater up over her head, her back forming a graceful arch as her arms rose, crossed and dispensed of the garment.

When she bent to shuck her jeans, he swallowed hard, taking in her profile, the slope of her breasts, the smooth plane of her stomach, curve of her hip. He told himself to look away, though he couldn't seem to do it.

For a second, he wondered which Lydia was real. The

leather-clad, tattooed temptress or the soft shadow of the woman hidden behind the curtains?

Was what had happened between them that night just another act, or had any of that been real? Ely shook his head hard, as if to break the spell. When he looked again, she'd moved away from the window. What was he doing here? Sometimes, there was a thin line between surveillance and Peeping Tom. Time to head out.

First, he walked back to the house, up to the porch. He didn't have to worry about leaving a path. His footsteps were sure to be buried beneath several feet of snow by morning.

Walking up to the door, he tugged on it to make sure it was locked—it was. He walked around and did the same to the back, finding it locked securely, as well.

Good.

He ran back to his truck and climbed in, turning on the heat. However, as he put it in Reverse, the visibility out the back windows was minimal and he misjudged the distance to the drainage ditch that ran along the side of the road. The next thing he knew, the back passenger side of the vehicle lurched down the slope.

Cursing, he knew he'd have to call for a tow. And it would probably be a while before they could get to him in this weather. He tried some more, rocking the truck back and forth, spinning the tires, and knowing he was probably only literally digging himself in deeper.

And figuratively, as well, since his options were few.

He called his driving association, only to have his suspicions confirmed. It would be a few hours before they could come pull him out; by then, it might be morning. In this snow, the truck would be buried. He told them to never mind.

He muttered another curse, wondering if he should

blow his cover with Lydia or walk back to town. Both had their dangers.

He returned to the house, looking up at the still-lit window, pondering his options. He really didn't have any. Walking unfamiliar roads back to town, at night, in this weather, was not smart. Resigned to his fate, he started to move to the porch, his inner alarm sounding just a few seconds too late. He wasn't alone.

He knew this primarily from the impression that a gun, very likely a double-barreled shotgun, was making against his spine.

"Enjoy standing around peeking in women's windows, huh?" someone said, and Ely tensed as he felt a little extra push from the nozzle of the gun.

"I wasn't making any trouble. I'm a friend of Lydia's," Ely said evenly. "I was coming over to check on her and make sure she was okay, but then my truck went off the road back near the entrance to the ranch."

"Really? So why not call for help?"

"I did. Tow trucks are busy tonight."

"You could have called Lydia. One of us would have come down with a winch, pulled you out. If you're such a friend and all."

Clearly the guy wasn't going to put the gun down, and Ely didn't blame him entirely.

"My name is Ely Berringer. I'm here from Philadelphia and I know Lydia from her shop, and she's best friends with my sister-in-law, but she doesn't know that I'm in town."

"Yeah, well, let's see what Lydia—or the sheriff—have to say about it."

Ely blew out a breath, knowing there was no way he could convince the guy to change his mind. He marched toward the house, with his hands still up, prodded by the

weapon pushed into his back. He could probably disarm
the man, but it was risky. Better to just let Lydia clear
up the misunderstanding.

Though she might tell the guy to shoot him, Ely
thought sardonically.

As the man knocked sharply on the door, Ely found
he was holding his breath again, wondering what Lydia's
reaction would be. His concern was short-lived as he
heard her yell, and then a shotgun blast echoed through
the night a few seconds later.

Ely ignored the push of the gun into his own back
as he snapped around, easily disarming his captor with
instincts and skill born of years of military training.
The other man fell to the porch floor with a grunt, un-
harmed. Ely took the weapon for himself and ran around
back of the house, his heart in his throat, unsure of what
he'd find when he got there.

LYDIA COULDN'T SLEEP even after she was ready for bed,
the events of the evening still replaying in her mind.
There'd been a few problems since she'd gotten back
into town, and maybe those cowboys coming after her
was a coincidence, but something in her gut told her
it wasn't.

The vet's report on the sick cow had been in the mail
when she'd come home tonight—the animal had been
poisoned. She was lucky it had only been one, and that
the cow would be fine.

The night after she had arrived, she'd found that a
message, Get Out, had been spray painted on her porch."

None too subtle there.

Horses had been let out of the barn at night that they
had to find before they froze to death, and she had been
mysteriously locked inside the garage while looking

for something of her father's. Luckily she'd been able to call for help before she had to drive her car through the door to escape. Then, some fencing had been destroyed on the back acres of the fields, and Smitty had had to spend two days fixing it.

Kyle said someone was trying to warn her off—no kidding. But she couldn't leave. She'd reported the incidents to a deputy who had dutifully written everything down, but said there was nothing he could do unless she caught someone in the act.

She wasn't even convinced that all of the events were connected. Maybe Smitty or Kyle had accidentally locked her in the garage, not knowing she was there, or forgotten to lock the barn, and had just not wanted to own up to it. Sportsmen on ATVs or snowmobiles, or even elk, sometimes crashed through fences. The spray painting, and the cow poisoning, however, were no joke.

If someone wanted her gone, all she could do was make it clear as possible that she would be out of here— in a few weeks.

Tonight, however, had been a completely different thing. Those cowboys had nothing good on their mind, and for the first time since she'd come home, she'd really felt unsafe. Ranches picked up temporary labor all the time, men passing through, looking for work, but something about those two men had seemed off. Like they didn't belong here.

She shook her head. How would she know? She didn't belong here anymore, either.

She forced herself to stop thinking about it by emptying one of the upstairs closets. She didn't want strangers going through her family's things. Besides, a hard look at her past would be a good reminder why she didn't belong here anymore, and why she could never belong to a guy like Ely.

It was a difficult enough task, physically and emotionally, to distract her somewhat from her troubles. In the middle of a box of photo albums, she pulled out her high school yearbook. Freshman year. Everything had been so different then, she thought. But so what? She'd had some bad breaks, but she'd recovered, right? Made something of herself. She had a good life, a new life, though somewhere down deep, she was never really sure if she deserved it.

Back then, she never would have questioned her future. She knew exactly what she'd wanted. To work the ranch, raise horses and have the same kind of life she'd known up until that point. She'd assumed she would marry one of the rodeo champs that she and her girl-friends had huge crushes on and have several pretty, well-behaved children. It was what most thirteen-year-old girls wanted. She turned to the back of the book, her eyes scanning the signatures until she found a familiar one.

Always be best of the best, Ginny.

Ginny had meant best of best friends. And they had been. Until that summer before their junior year when everything had changed. Life had changed, and all their pretty, perfect dreams had evaporated in one cruel slam of fate. But it hadn't been fate—it had been Lydia's fault. None of it would have happened if not for her.

Lydia sucked in a breath, closing the book sharply. She sat there on the side of her mother's bed, looking around her at a lifetime's collection of memories and… stuff. There was so much to go through. How was she supposed to do this by herself? She could barely get through one closet. But the idea of anyone else going through it was unbearable. Besides, there was no one else. She was on her own, like she'd been for a long time.

Putting the book down, she blocked out her worry and lay back on the bed. Tomorrow, she'd come up with a plan for dealing with it all. Right now, she was too overwhelmed and exhausted to think of anything.

Sleep crept over her before she had a chance to get back up, change or make her way to her own room. In her dreams, she was with Ginny, playing and laughing under broad, blue Montana skies.

That summer after their freshman year in high school had been perfect and full of promise. The images ran through Lydia's mind like an old slide presentation, but it all felt real, making her smile in her sleep.

Then abruptly there was noise, a rush of hooves and screams, and the eerie beeping of some machine by the side of Ginny's hospital bed. Lydia sat with her friend, who, when she awakened, stared at Lydia accusingly.

"Why would you do this to me?" Ginny said, and then turned her face away, other angry voices chiming in. *How could you do this? What were you thinking? You ruined her life forever, you selfish little bitch.*

Guilt sliced Lydia to her bones, because she knew they were right. Footsteps pounded loud somewhere behind her; a nurse, or someone coming to tell her she had no right to be there. Not after what she'd done. *Get out. If you're smart, you'll never come back.*

Lydia awoke with a start, curled up on the bed, the light still on, tears coursing from her eyes.

Dammit.

The nightmares had stopped years ago, though she never really forgot. Being here brought it all back in stark, painful color.

So did the fear that followed her every time she

went into town, worry that she would bump into one of Ginny's family and have to face it all over again. The recrimination, the blame. Her mother said it was all in the past, and that Ginny was doing fine. That she had married, gotten on with her life.

Really? How fine could she be, paralyzed from the waist down, her dreams shattered?

Lydia was glad if Ginny had managed to find some happiness, but that didn't make what she had done any more forgivable. It was why she had to get out of here as soon as she could wrap up her obligations. She didn't like living with all these ghosts; this was all in the past and it had to be left there.

Looking at the clock through bleary eyes, she saw she had only dozed off for less than a half hour, and she was intent on doing more work. It had to be done if she was getting out of here.

She froze as a sound traveled up from the first floor. Footsteps.

She'd heard them in her dream, too, but now she was awake. Had she imagined it? These were heavy, hard and making their way through the bottom floor.

Holding her breath, she walked carefully to the edge of the door and heard the squeak that came from the floorboard between the dining room and the kitchen.

She wasn't imagining it. Someone was down there. She thought she heard some voices, as well. Male voices.

Smitty? Kyle? But why would they be in the house in the middle of the night? Had the cowboys who'd harassed her earlier followed her home, or found out where she lived? But she had locked the doors; made sure to do so. Suddenly Clear River was feeling a lot more dangerous than south Philly.

Another crash made her jump, and she knew she had

to do something. Slipping from the room, she edged down the hall to the stairs. At the end of the hall was her father's gun rack; his favorite shotgun was still there.

Holding her breath, she made it to the gun rack, and retrieved the weapon. Her intruder's footsteps were only yards away, traversing the kitchen. Lydia held her breath and moved in that direction. Stopping just outside the kitchen, she swallowed with resolve and snapped the barrel of the gun into place. Silence.

"I have a gun, and if you're not out of this house in two seconds, I'll use it," she warned, her voice more steady than she would have expected. She turned the corner of the kitchen just in time to see someone duck outside the back door.

She took chase, yelling after them. When she reached the back door, she fired up into the air, hoping to shock them, to perhaps see who it was.

But the shadowy intruder disappeared into the trees.

Or so she thought.

She tried to load the gun again, but no go—it had only had one shell.

No matter, it was yanked from her hands a second later as she stumbled back into the kitchen, trying to get away. She went sprawling. A sharp pain stabbed at her hand, but she ignored it as she scrambled to find another weapon, anything within reach.

"Lydia."

She didn't listen, panic frying her brain.

"Lydia, stop. It's me, Ely."

The words finally permeated her brain, and she stopped her frantic dash across the floor, as the lights flicked on.

"Lydia, are you okay? What happened?" Kyle.

Ely and Kyle, she mentally recited.

Was she still dreaming? Ely and Kyle seemed so surreal.

But it was real.

Ely held her shotgun and a second one. Handing both to Kyle, he bent down, picking her up from the floor like she weighed nothing.

"Lydia, it's okay," he said gently and pulled her in close.

A weak moment, she would tell herself later. Right now, Ely was the most solid thing she'd felt in days. Weeks. She allowed herself to curl into the safety and support he offered, just for a minute. God, he felt good.

Everyone was quiet until she looked down and saw the blood soaking into the material of his sweat jacket.

"You're hurt," she whispered.

Ely looked down, frowning, and then cursed, taking her arm in his hand.

"No, that would be you," he said.

She looked down and saw he was right. Her hand was bleeding where she had cut it on something on the floor. She took in the sight of the wrecked kitchen, and her knees wavered a little.

"Sit," Ely commanded, leading her to a chair.

Ely was quiet as he examined her hand.

"It's not bad, just bleeding a lot. You have a first-aid kit around here anywhere?"

Kyle, still watching them closely, put the guns down and went to her kitchen cupboard, pulling out a small, white box.

Lydia shook her head. She wouldn't have known that was there. Kyle knew her house better than she did. Well, he had been here all this time, and she had not been.

"I guess we had better call the sheriff, after all," Ely said.

"I followed whoever it was out to the tree line before I came in, but he was gone," Kyle muttered agreement.

"No, don't call anyone," Lydia interrupted.

Ely looked at her in surprise. "Someone broke into your house, wrecked the place. You need to report it."

She shook her head. They wouldn't do anything anyway, as she already knew.

"It would be a waste of time. I didn't see who did it, and the authorities are probably busy with the storm. It's probably just someone who thought the house was empty, or some kids out looking for excitement or something. They took off the minute I let them know I was here, so they didn't mean me any harm," she said, maybe a little desperately. Who was she trying to convince?

"Or whoever it was could be the one who's been giving you trouble since you got here, and—"

Lydia cut Kyle off with a sharp look.

"Lydia—"

"Why are you here?" she whispered, interrupting him.

She knew everything was a wreck around her, and she couldn't deal with that. Not just yet. So she focused on him.

"Tessa sent me. She wanted to make sure you were okay."

Lydia's eyes closed, and she shook her head.

"When you came up the side of the house, I thought you were—"

"I know. I'm sorry. My truck is stuck back on the road, and Kyle caught me out front of the house. He thought I might be trouble. We were just sorting it out when we heard the gun go off. And who's been giving you trouble?"

"Not sure, but they—"

"Kyle, we're fine," Lydia interrupted him again with a direct look. "Why don't you head back down to the bunkhouse, and I'll see you in the morning."

Ely's gaze narrowed on her, but he didn't say a word.

Lydia's pretty mouth flattened into a line of displeasure as she looked at Kyle.

"So I did see you earlier," she said. "In town."

He nodded.

"You do know each other? From back east?" Kyle asked, still not moving.

"That's right." Exhausted, her hand throbbing, Lydia felt a chill travel over her skin. She was clad only in the robe she had put on after undressing, having become distracted by her thoughts and cleaning out the closet. Pulling the fabric more tightly around herself, she was aware of being far too exposed, especially with Ely pressing against her leg as he bandaged her hand. She shivered.

"We're…friends, yes. It's okay, Kyle, really. Good-night."

Kyle nodded, grabbed his rifle and headed back out the door. Lydia shook her head as Ely packed up the small first-aid kit and returned it to the cabinet. She took the moment to test her legs and stood up, feeling steadier, as she glanced around.

"I can't believe someone would do this," she said, more to herself than to him. Bowls and dishes that had been on the counter were broken all over the floor—it was a miracle that she hadn't cut herself when she had went running through the kitchen after her intruder.

"What's been going on, Lydia? You just pick up and leave Philly, and now you're being harassed, twice in one night?"

Something about his making demands quickly set her spine on edge. She turned, nailing him with a glare.

"I think you're the one who has some explaining to do. How did you know where I lived, and how come you were here so late at night? Have you been following me?"

"I only got here yesterday, but it was enough time to check the town records, yes, and find out where you lived."

"I don't live here."

"You did," he challenged. "Why the big secret?"

She swallowed, overly aware of him as they stood facing each other, the slight swath of cotton that she wore hardly enough to make her feel adequately covered. He seemed to notice as well, his eyes taking her in briefly before returning to her face. He didn't say anything, but she saw the flicker of memory, of desire. Her body responded as well, her chill wearing off as her blood heated a little. She ignored it.

"I have to get dressed and take care of this mess."

"You're really not going to report the break-in?"

She didn't respond, walking out of the room, leaving Ely behind. Maybe he'd take the hint and leave.

Probably not. She heard a cupboard open and close, and it sounded like he was starting to clean up.

Great. The last thing she needed right now was Ely trying to be her white knight.

She took a few minutes to get her bearings and to get some clothes on. She also had to process the fact that Ely Berringer was down in her kitchen, as real as the day was long, all sexy, muscle-bound, six-foot-something of him. The universe sure did enjoy toying with her.

If she thought her life was complicated an hour ago, now that word had taken on an entirely new meaning.

3

ELY TOOK OFF HIS wet hoodie and boots, putting them out in the mudroom. He had picked up a good deal of the mess on the floor before wondering if Lydia was coming back. Maybe she fell back asleep. Did she hit her head when she'd fallen?

Concerned, he put down the broom and walked out into the hall, admiring the solid beams along the ceiling and hardwood floors. The wood was worn and aged in that way that only made it more attractive, and the place had a homey feeling about it. New construction was never this solid anymore. He went upstairs and saw the light shining from under a closed door. Knocking softly, he asked, "Lydia, are you okay?"

She mumbled something, but was definitely awake.

"Do you need help? Should I come in?"

"No," she barked.

Okay, he thought, retreating from the door. That was clear enough.

Making his way back downstairs, he looked around, fully intending to go and check on her whether she liked it or not if she didn't materialize in the next five minutes.

As he waited, he took the place in. Family pictures crowded the walls, which were covered with a bold William Morris wallpaper. An interesting choice. He only knew about the style because his mother was wild for anything from the Arts and Crafts movement. Their father had sharpened their interests in technology and sports, but their mother had insisted that her boys have some sense of art in the world.

She'd taken Ely and his brothers to museums and to every Arts and Crafts movement exhibit that came along. She'd even brought them on weekend trips to visit Falling Water, Oak Park and other Frank Lloyd Wright destinations.

He had to admit, the four of them hadn't always been enthusiastic participants, but she'd made it fun and the experience had stayed with him as he reached adulthood. When he'd gotten his own place after coming home from the Middle East, he'd sought out many of the natural designs his mother also preferred, finding them soothing to his battle-weary spirit.

She would love this house, which had definite aspects of Prairie construction, though it was more of a mélange of different styles that all came together.

The rooms were large, with low ceilings and warm colors. Large windows allowed for a lot of light, but were also a challenge to the heating bill, he imagined. If you stood too close to a window, you could feel the chill.

The yellow kitchen was huge, more of a typical farmhouse style with a large, solid wood chopping block island near the sink, and a cool Formica table closer to the entry. The floor needed some work. Rather than wood, the floor in there was old linoleum, and as he walked through, he noticed some points where it was sinking. Probably needed supports in the basement.

There could be some foundation problems, as well. The house was warm, but there was a draft, and he noted that someone had put plastic over the kitchen windows. It wasn't doing much good.

He busied himself by making mental notes of some less obvious wear-and-tear issues, things that would need to be repaired before Lydia could sell the place. He stopped as he encountered a wall in the dining room, one full of family pictures.

Lydia as a baby, Lydia on a horse, smiling a girlie grin that was missing one tooth—she couldn't be more than six. Ely found himself smiling at the picture of a slightly older Lydia with her parents by the Christmas tree, and another dressed as a cheerleader—a cheerleader? Ely's mind boggled.

She'd been cute—a smiling, happy young woman who showed hints of the sexy charm that would develop later. Her blue eyes were open and happy; unlike now, when she was often guarded and distant.

One picture of her as a teen was with another girl her age, their arms thrown around each other, a birthday cake bright with candles in front of them as they both threw kisses to the camera.

As he reached up to get a closer look at one of the photos, a hard case fell from the table to the floor. He picked it up, his eyebrows rising at the name of the artist on the cover of the CD.

Jack Johnson. He replaced it, noticing a few others, all soft rock, country or easy listening.

A lot different than the hard metal music that Lydia tended to play in the shop; that stuff gave him a headache. On the inside of one case, someone had written:

Our little secret. Happy Birthday, Tessa.

Another one was a birthday gift.

It all presented a confusing—but intriguing—image.

Lydia, the woman who was covered in ink, piercings, who wore leather and listened to thrash metal and enjoyed one-nighters that included an array of kinky sex toys, was also a wholesome country girl who had grown up on a farm with horses, cows and who enjoyed easy-listening music and reading?

"I see you're making yourself at home," she said from behind him.

He turned to find her leaning against a doorjamb, fully dressed again. Black jeans, black T-shirt with some symbol painted on the front. She looked more like herself—the self that he was familiar with—though she still wore no makeup. He liked it better that way, actually. She seemed even sexier than he remembered, and what he remembered was plenty sexy.

"I started cleaning up, but I was concerned when you didn't come back down. Are you okay?"

She shrugged. "Fine."

The mask was back in place. She still looked pale, tired. Wary. Pissed off.

"It's a beautiful old house," he said, taking the room in again. "You grew up here."

It was a statement, not a question. She didn't answer.

"I was really sorry to find out about your mother, Lydia. Are you doing okay?"

She shrugged again, unwilling to give, and he was unsure what he was supposed to do, so he turned back to the wall.

"Who's the other girl in this birthday photo?"

"You shouldn't be here," she said sharply.

There it was. Might as well get it over with now.

"If it wasn't me, it would have been Tessa. She was worried sick about you."

He saw the flash of guilt in her eyes, and she looked down at the floor as she responded. "I know. I meant to get in contact with her, but it's been busy."

"Too busy to let her know you were okay? Where you were? Or too worried that she'd find out everything you told her about your life before Philly was a lie?"

Straightening, Lydia took a step into the room. "I don't need to explain any of this to you or to anyone, for that matter. You had no right to poke around in my life. My mother died. I'm here to settle everything, and that's no one's business but mine. Why would you care anyway? I thought you were off…somewhere."

Ely took a step closer, too, feeling the draw. He figured if he'd come this far, he might as well go the rest of the way. As he moved in, he picked up the clean scent of her soap and shampoo and his body hummed with recognition.

"Why did you leave? You look happy, in these pictures. What happened?"

"Nothing. I just needed to get out. What are you going to tell Tessa?"

"I'm not sure yet. I need to let her know you're okay, at least."

Lydia frowned.

"Or you could do that yourself. I don't need to tell her anything."

"I'd prefer if you didn't. It's not your place."

He nodded. She was right about that.

"What did Kyle mean about someone causing you trouble?"

Lydia rolled her eyes. "Kyle has an active imagination."

"I don't think so. What's been going on?"

"I'm serious. Don't go playing bodyguard on me, Ely. Nothing is going on."

They stood, closer now, facing off, and Ely was getting tired of the verbal thrust and parry. He had to curl his fingers in to stop from touching her. Or shaking her. She was stubborn and seemed set against giving in. Or just intent to give him a hard time.

It wasn't enough to make him want to let her off the hook. If she was in trouble, he wanted to know.

"I won't leave until I know for sure, Lydia," he said calmly and saw anger flicker in the depths of her eyes. It traveled down to her cheeks and blossomed there. When she licked her lips before speaking, his response was sharp and true, like a shot of adrenaline through his system.

"Fine, whatever," she said, throwing her hands up and walking into the kitchen. He took a deep breath and followed.

She paused at the entry, taking in the room. "Thanks for cleaning up—you didn't need to do all that." She sounded surprised.

"I didn't mind. It looked personal, if you want my opinion. Strangers might steal something, or look for valuables, but this was more like someone wants to scare you. Or send a message. So again, who would do this? Or at least, why?"

"Maybe it was those guys from earlier who followed me back here," she said as she grabbed a teakettle from the stove.

Ely shook his head. "No one followed you back. I made sure."

"How could you? Where is your truck?" she said, yet again avoiding his question.

"Down the road, in a ditch."

"I didn't see you following me," she said, frowning.

"I'm really good at it."

She paused. "You won't be able to get to it now. The snow's coming down too hard. There are two extra rooms upstairs, or you can have the couch."

She came to the table with two glasses of hot, black tea, setting one down in front of him. Ely didn't really care for tea, but he picked it up and took a sip anyway. Glancing down at the expanse of her ankle exposed when she crossed one leg over the other, he was distracted by both the fuzzy pink slippers that she wore and the tattooed vine that wound around her ankle and calf. He knew that it continued up the length of her smooth thigh, providing a path to the sweetest bit of sin he'd ever known.

"It's not as bad as I thought. Whoever it was didn't break any of the important stuff," she said.

"Important stuff?"

"Yeah, like those yellowware bowls on the counter—they are probably close to one hundred years old. Or the antique glass in that cupboard. Those were my mother's favorites, all Depression-Era, some very valuable. They ripped some random stuff out of the cupboards, the dinner plates we always use, even the dirty ones in the sink. Nothing valuable. Strange, but lucky, I guess."

"They just wanted to make noise, shake you up."

"Well, they succeeded, at least for a minute or two," she said, blowing out a breath. "But I think you and Kyle are wrong. It was probably just teens out looking for a rush."

"In this storm? In the middle of the week, way out here? The house has been empty for weeks, and just now they decide to come in and trash it?" Ely argued. "People know you are here—it's a small town. I assume

word spreads fast. So, what kind of trouble are you in?"
he asked, cutting to the chase.

Lydia leveled a cool stare back at him.

"I don't need to be rescued, Ely. Thanks, anyway."

Ely set his cup down. He could be stubborn, too.

"Well, if someone is bothering you, this time they
came inside your house, Lydia, while you were at home,
sleeping. That's not harmless teenage harassment, or
some kind of coincidence. It means they're willing to es-
calate the situation if you don't do something to stop it."

"I am going to do something about it. I'm going to
leave, as soon as I can," she said calmly, shaking her
head as she indirectly admitted to him that there had
been a problem.

Her hands betrayed her cool tone; they trembled
slightly when she picked up her tea. She wasn't as in-
different as she was pretending to be.

"You might as well hit the sack so you can get up
early and have Kyle pull your truck out, so you can
leave."

Ely nearly smiled at her bluntness.

"Not until I know you're okay. Tessa would have
my head. Maybe I should stay here until you go back
to Philly. Keep an eye on things."

She stood, looking almost as panicked as she had
earlier.

"No, I don't think so."

"I'm technically still on vacation, and it's a nice
town. I've never been to Montana. Seems like as nice
a place to spend Christmas as anywhere."

"Why are you doing this? Just leave me alone," she
said tightly. "I don't know if you have some fantasy
about saving me, or thinking we're going to continue

what we had that night, but we're not. It was a one-night thing, Ely, that's it."

Before she could turn away from him, pushing him away, he spun her around to face him. She was under a lot of stress at the moment, taking a lot of emotional hits at once. Ely knew that people reacted to grief differently, and Lydia apparently didn't like accepting help from anyone under the best of circumstances, let alone in situations that made her especially vulnerable.

"It's not about that. I know exactly what that was, don't worry. You need someone, whether you're too pigheaded to know it or not."

"Well, I don't need you," she said, pushing away from him.

Her words hit him hard. "Really?"

The next thing he knew, he was kissing her.

She tasted so good, he lost himself almost immediately. At first she didn't kiss him back, her hands planted against his chest. If she had resisted for one more second, he would have stopped.

But she didn't. In the next minute her arms slid upward and she wound herself around him like the tattooed vine that wrapped itself around her exquisite body. She opened to him, letting him in.

Letting him close in this way, if not any other.

He'd take it. Her arms were tight around his neck as he plunged deeper, tasted more.

Lydia dug her nails into his shoulders, moaning against him, and Ely didn't know anything else, only that it felt damned good.

APPARENTLY, ELY didn't care for her brush-off. When he'd crowded her up against the counter, Lydia tried to push him back, but the minute her hands landed on his chest, her traitorous fingers had curled into the material of his damp shirt. He'd looked at her so strangely before he'd kissed her, his expression a mix of emotions she couldn't identify as she wrestled with her own. He hadn't liked her saying that she didn't need him. Frustration, certainly. Stubbornness, and maybe even a slight hint of hurt.

He parted her lips wide with his own, giving her little choice in the matter as his tongue sliding over hers, tempting—no, daring—her to come out and play. Lydia reacted from sheer need and adrenaline, all of the desperate wanting she'd ignored for two months surging into the kiss as she dug her fingers into his hair, giving as good as she got. She might not need him, but she needed *this*—this blinding passion, the heat that erased everything but the kiss. Mouths mating violently, the intensity burned a clean path through her heart, leaving only Ely and her desire for him in its wake.

Desire, she could deal with. Desire was easy and uncomplicated.

He pulled back, only to bury his face at her throat, proceeding to drive her crazy with his tongue and teeth on her skin, his hands traveling under her shirt, closing over her breasts with a moan. She pressed into his touch, urging him on.

His arms slid to her back, banding around her as she tugged on his hair to bring his mouth back to her lips. They didn't need air for quite some time as the kiss went on and on. This made more sense than any of their words did.

Hard against her hip, he ground into the soft, hot apex of her thighs, pushing her close to the edge. He was close, too. When she reached down, closing her hand over the steely ridge at the front of his jeans, he shuddered from head to toe.

She could take him upstairs. Sate herself and forget everything that was complicating her life for another night. It sounded like the best idea she'd had in days.

"Too many clothes," she whispered, her voice shaking with need. He had her so close to coming, all it would take was a sweet bit of pressure in just the right spot and it would be all over.

Taking in his darkened eyes and ragged breathing, she knew that he was in the same shape. But Lydia had too much experience to mistake lust for anything more.

"I'm sorry. I didn't come here to do that," he said, walking away from her to the other side of the kitchen, pushing his hands through his hair. He turned to meet her gaze with his own, still smoldering with banked desire.

Lydia blew out a breath, wondering what she had been thinking. Well, she hadn't been. That had been a close call. Ely wasn't the kind of guy who got involved casually, and that was all Lydia did. This would have been another mistake.

"You're right. No apology needed."

She had a feeling that he never meant for her to find out he was here. He'd been watching her and reporting back. The fact that they were here in her kitchen together was an accident that was never supposed to happen. She couldn't let herself be fooled. No doubt he wanted to help; helping was his *job*.

And she had made a fool out of herself, almost taking him to bed, again.

He backed away as sanity returned in small bits to both of them. The distance was both a relief and…not.

"I don't know what got into me, but you just…" He

shook his head, and she wondered what he was about to say.

"I know. Me, too. It's just been a crazy night, that's all. Listen, why don't we get some sleep, and then I can make you breakfast and the guys can help you get the truck out so you can be on your way. I'm okay here on my own, Ely. Seriously."

"Make me breakfast? You cook?" he said lightly, teasingly, trying to lighten the mood between them.

"I like to cook, actually," she said, trying to meet him halfway. To sound normal, as if nothing had happened. As if they hadn't almost swallowed each other whole right here in the kitchen where she used to bake Christmas cookies as a girl.

"Yeah?"

"My mother taught me. We always had a garden, fresh foods. Beef and dairy, of course. I sometimes cook dinner at my place, invite all of my friends over."

"Really?" he said softly, looking at her, the heat burning off, but still evident in his face and in the way he held his body. "And here I thought I was one of your friends."

That set her back. Ely, a friend?

"Why would you think that?" she asked baldly, and saw the surprise register in his face. She wasn't known for her subtlety, but that had been rude, even for her. "I'm sorry. It's just that, that one night aside, we really don't know each other well. And it wasn't like you hung around for long after the wedding."

She sighed, looking outside where the snow whipped against the windows even harder than it had been before, and she shook her head. Her luck he couldn't just leave now.

"You're right. But maybe we could fix all that. Let me help, Lydia."

"Don't do this, Ely."

"What?"

"Charm me. Seduce me. Wheedle your way through my defenses. Try to get what you want by working your way into my life somehow. Protect me. Whatever else you have in mind," she said, turning to the sink to wash her hands. "You can stay tonight, and then you need to go home."

"That sounds familiar," he said, a little edge to his voice. "I just want to help with whatever trouble you're having now. Be a friend. Is that so bad?"

She turned to face him, and he met her eyes.

"Really? That's all?"

"I won't lie. I've thought about that night a lot since it happened. You…that night we had, it inspired me to really think about my life and what I want out of it."

She frowned. "How?"

"Well, for one, I think I dodged a bullet with Chloe, though I didn't know it at the time. And meeting you, seeing how freely you enjoy life, how spontaneous and unfettered you are, it made me wonder why I'm so anxious to always tie myself down. I've been tied to something for my entire life—my family, the Marines, Berringer's. Those things are important to me, but I need some…freedom, I guess. You showed me that."

She was speechless. Stunned.

"I don't understand. I thought that you were ashamed of being with me," she blurted.

He looked clearly taken aback. "Whoa. Hold on a second there. I wasn't ashamed of anything. Why would you think that?"

"You avoided me like the plague. You barely spoke

to me, danced with everyone at Tessa and Jonas's wedding but me," she said hotly, then slapped a hand over her mouth, hating that she had let that hurtful bit slip.

Dammit. She was tired, and stretched to her last nerve, otherwise she never would have said that. Too late now.

"Hell, Lydia. I thought that was how you wanted it, for no one to know. I didn't mean to hurt you. That wasn't my intention. I guess I overdid it, trying to act like nothing had happened. I was pretty screwed up to start with, and afterward, I felt like a jerk for using Tessa's best friend to forget my troubles for a night. You deserve better than that. So I kept my distance."

Lydia pushed a hand through her hair. She'd never made an effort or tried to talk to him about it, either. They'd both made a mess of it.

"It shouldn't matter—it doesn't matter—but I just thought you didn't want anyone to know that the big, brave Marine had gotten down and dirty with the Goth girl. I guess that got to me a little."

He swore. "I didn't mean it that way. I never thought that for a moment. I'm so sorry."

Lydia wasn't sure how to feel about his confession, but they'd aired it out and now she wanted to move past it.

"So now you're a free agent? Not looking for the white picket fences anymore?" she asked.

He smiled. "Not anytime soon. I was trying too hard, rushing it. Why get tied down? At least, not in a relationship," he said, the light in his eyes telling her that getting tied down in other ways was much more likely.

Lydia's mind was spinning, and she turned to pick up something that had been left on the floor, needing a moment.

So what he had taken from their night together was that he wanted to be free to be with as many women as he felt like, do whatever he wanted, with no strings?

Why did that bother her so much? It was how she'd lived her life for the last twelve years. How she *still* lived her life.

Maybe it was because she knew he didn't really mean it. Men like Ely didn't change their stripes overnight. He believed in commitment, he'd been raised to believe in it, and he wanted it for himself. She'd seen it at the wedding, how he watched his parents with such open affection, and how happy he was for Jonas and Tessa. And because of how wrecked he'd been when he found out his ex had duped him.

It's how he lived his life. Who he was to his core. He might be taking a little break from that, but ultimately, Ely was a long-term kind of guy.

"So what do you want now, Ely?"

"I want to help," he said easily. "I know you need someone who can work on this place so you can sell it."

She turned to look at him sharply. "And how do you know—ah, right, you were following me today." He would have seen all of her failed attempts to find contractors to hire.

"If you want to unload this place, it needs some fixing up. I can help with that."

She frowned, crossing her arms in front of her.

"Are you serious?"

"I am. If you want to pay for materials, the labor is free. No strings. And in case anything else happens, I'm close by."

"That's all?"

He stepped in closer. "I don't know. Maybe we could

stay open to anything else? No pressure and no expectations. But we're good together."

"No strings?"

"Nope." He shook his head resolutely. "No rules, no commitments—except for being friends," he said, reaching to push some hair back behind her ear. "That would be nice for when we both have to go back to Philly."

Lydia chewed her lip, considering. She needed to unload this place, and the house needed work. He was the solution to her problem. It surprised her, really, how much she wanted to agree. And if he meant it, if it was just to help out, to be a friend, then maybe it could work.

"What happens when we go back to Philly?"

He shrugged. "We'll be friends. We'll go back to our lives, I guess. See each other when our paths cross."

"What are you going to tell Tessa?"

"I'll tell her I found you, you're fine, and I'm stuck out here in the weather for a few days. The rest is yours to tell. Or not."

Lydia felt enormous relief that he wasn't going to tell Tessa about what he knew. If letting him stay here and help would prevent him from revealing her secrets to her friend, and help her get the house in shape, she'd be an idiot not to agree—and Lydia wasn't an idiot.

It was an enormous temptation, as well, to give in to his other offer, but that could be risky—maybe even more so if he meant it, the no-strings bit. She wasn't sure anymore if she could do that. Not when it came to Ely, and with her life so upside down.

Maybe, this time, they could find a way to be friends. They had chemistry, sure, but that didn't mean they had to act on it, right?

"I could use help fixing things up," she relented. "If you really know what you're doing."

Ely nodded, relaxing. "I do. We can talk about it in the morning. So where do you want me to sleep?" he asked, clearly wondering about the other side of his proposition.

She frowned. "Not with me. I think we could just try being friends. Not that I'm not tempted, but I have so much going on, and—"

He shushed her gently. "No problem. That's perfectly okay. Whatever you need, Lydia."

She smiled, not sure if she was relieved or not at his easy acceptance of her rejection. But it was for the best.

"If you don't mind, maybe I could catch a hot shower and some shut-eye?" he asked, turning away.

Lydia blinked with how quickly they'd gone from fighting to kissing to this casual agreement. Was she fooling herself that she could have him around and maintain her distance? Was he fooling himself? No. He was straighter than an arrow, and she was stronger than that.

"Sure, the shower's upstairs, straight down the hall on the left. The beds in the other room aren't made up, so if you want to take the sofa, that's fine. It's pretty comfortable. I can make up a room for you tomorrow."

The idea of him in her shower was filling her mind with lust.

"I can stay in the bunkhouse, if you want," he offered.

"I'm not sure what the accommodations are like down there anymore. There's more than enough room here, and if you're working on the house, it makes sense," she said easily, as if it would be no problem at all.

"Okay, then, thanks. See you in the morning," he said casually, as if they were pals, hanging out. Easy-peasy.

When he left, she felt as if she had been picked up and landed down somewhere else, completely disoriented. Had she really gone from not wanting him here to agreeing to let him stay and help her with the house?

It all seemed so reasonable.

She picked up their empty mugs and found herself tracing the edge of the cup he had drunk from, remembering the touch of his lips and his hands. Realizing what she was doing, she put the mug down so quickly she almost broke it, and cursed under her breath.

How did he manage to turn her inside out so easily without seeming like he even suffered a hair out of place? It didn't matter. They'd talked, kissed, and would part ways this time as…friends.

That still didn't feel quite right, but it would make things easier when they went back to Philly. She shut off the lights and headed to bed, trying not to listen to the water running in the shower down the hall from her room. Thinking about him naked in her shower, the hot water running over all of those lovely muscles. She pretended not to notice that the door had opened a bit. A gentle invitation?

Tempting as it was, she walked into her room, shutting the door tight. Ely might think he was happy playing things free and easy, but she knew that giving in would only make things more difficult. Right now, that was the last thing she needed.

4

ELY FELT GREAT in spite of his lack of sleep the night before. He'd showered and hit the sofa, but had no expectation of sleep. Not with Lydia in her room upstairs. In her bed.

He couldn't help but peek into the room she was using—her bags were all over the place—and she'd left the door wide open. Needless to say, the decor here was very different than her bedroom back in Philly, which was part BDSM parlor, part French boudoir.

Here, pretty watercolors hung on the walls by the bed. In her apartment, erotic black-and-whites adorned the walls of the room. The sheets in this warm-toned room were cotton, soft and comforting. There were handmade quilts on the bed.

Back home, Lydia preferred satin. They'd been scarlet red the night he'd been with her.

Needless to say, with those memories and their kiss on his mind, sleep was not going to happen. He hadn't come here thinking about sleeping with Lydia again—quite the opposite—but after he'd kissed her, he'd hoped she might change her mind. Let him make it up to her for being such a jerk before. He hadn't meant to hurt her, but apparently, he'd done a good enough job of it that she wasn't interested in a second go-round. That was fine, he told himself, ignoring the mocking chant in the back of his brain that said he was fooling himself.

So he'd spent a couple of hours making a list of things he'd need to start making repairs. The wiring was old but should pass inspection, he thought, but it wouldn't hurt to replace several sockets and the old fixtures. The bigger jobs would be shoring up the kitchen floor and doing something with the windows. He wasn't sure if she wanted to replace the windows, or if that could even be done in a timely way, but they could recaulk and perhaps insulate them better.

He dressed and left early, the rumbling of a motor outside waking him before it was light. Not that there would be much light with the storm still dumping snow by the buckets. Predawn gave way to just a slightly less-dark morning. Smitty, the ranch manager, an older man about sixty or so, was starting up a tractor with a plow attachment outside the larger barn.

"Need an extra pair of hands?"

Smitty looked him in the eye, and nodded. "You that friend of Lydia's that Kyle mentioned?"

"That would be me," Ely said, offering a handshake and then going to work alongside the man. "I'll be around for a few days, and don't mind helping out."

"Good to know."

Ely grabbed a shovel to start clearing the more narrow paths as Smitty plowed the main areas between the house and the barns. Kyle emerged, heading directly to the barn without talking to either of them. He sent a glare in Ely's direction, and Ely casually saluted back before Kyle disappeared into the barn.

The morning became a bit brighter, and Lydia came out to join them, offering only a grumbling good morning as she walked by. Not so much a morning person, he guessed.

Ely continued to work, enjoying the brisk air, though he wished he had his heavier jacket with him. The effort kept him warm, more or less, but when a wind blew, it cut through his light coat.

A ringing came from his pocket, and he pulled out his phone.

Jonas.

"Hey, brother."

"Ely. What's going on? Tessa won't stop pacing, so I promised I'd call and get a status report."

"Sorry about that. I was going to call her today, but we got hit by a storm, so we're in the process of digging out. The white stuff is still coming down."

"I didn't call for a weather report," Jonas said sarcastically, in his usual gruff style. Tessa had done a lot to soften him up, but he was still Jonas. "Are you okay? And Lydia?"

"Yeah. She's fine, but I might stick around for a while just to make sure. My truck went off the road last night, so I ended up staying at her place."

"Her place? How does Lydia have a place in Montana?"

Ely gave his brother the skinniest version of the truth that he could. "But I'd rather you didn't tell Tessa any of that. Lydia wants to tell her herself when she comes home."

Hopefully, Ely thought uncomfortably.

"I see. So until then, you're staying with her at this ranch? Just the two of you?"

"It's not what you think, Jon. And there are ranch hands around, as well."

"I know how it can be to be stuck in a storm with a beautiful woman," Jonas said with a chuckle. "Changed my whole life."

Tess and Jonas had been stuck in a major east coast storm the previous summer, one that caused blackouts up and down the entire seaboard. Jonas had lost his eyesight, and he and Tessa ended up traversing the city in the storm in order to help one of her elderly friends. It had been a tense time, but it was also when they had fallen in love.

Ely needed Jonas to know the same thing did not apply in this case. Even if he and Lydia had agreed to be friends for the time being, it was never going to come to more than that. He had his whole life ahead of him, and he wasn't going to go jumping into another serious relationship.

"Listen, I'm helping her out with a few things here, especially since I can't get out anyway, but that's all there is to it."

"That's it? You're sure?"

"Yeah. That's it. I did a crappy thing to her back in the fall, and I know it. I wasn't thinking straight then, and I need to make it right, so that's what I'm doing now."

That, at least, was the truth.

"Tessa will be disappointed. I think she was still holding out hope you and Lydia would get together."

"You'd think she'd know Lydia better than that, and I'm not in any rush to get involved in anything, either. If I learned anything back in the fall, it was that I am not ready to be in any kind of committed relationship at this point."

"Who are you trying to convince, Ely?"

"Bite me, Jonas. And even if you don't believe me, you know how Lydia is."

"Yeah, I know. I tried to tell Tessa that, too. Lydia doesn't do relationships, but she does a lot of other things," Jonas recited with a chuckle, and Ely froze in place.

"How would you know about that? Did you guys ever—"

"No way. Lydia says that to everyone—it's her personal motto, but also kind of a joke between friends. Believe me, Lydia's way too scary for me to think about, uh, well, you know. I love her like a sister, so I'm glad you two are making nice, but no. She and I never went there, not even in my head," Jonas said with a shudder of sorts.

Ely laughed, partly from relief and partly from his brother's adamant refusal. He knew Jonas had gotten close to Lydia while he'd been protecting Tessa, but Ely was glad to know it hadn't been *that* close.

"Sounds to me like you wouldn't care for someone else getting to know her that well, though. Make sure you do have your head on straight, Ely."

"It is, don't worry. Maybe for the first time in a long time."

"How was Antigua?"

"Heaven."

"In other words, completely the opposite of Montana?"

"You got that right," he said, looking around at the snow. "Tell Tessa everything is okay, and Lydia will be in touch. But in the meantime, not to worry. We're okay here."

"Okay," Jonas agreed. "She'll want to know more,

but I'll tell her Lydia will talk to her when she gets back."

Ely agreed, and the brothers said goodbye. He looked around, taking in the scenery around him. He'd been joking when he told Jonas that Montana was so far from heaven. He loved the Caribbean, the blue waters and long beaches. But here, the air was clean and brisk, and he felt…free. It really was Big Sky Country, and his spirit responded to that with energy he hadn't felt in a long time. He loved wide-open spaces, and had forgotten that after being in the city for so long.

Removing the mountains of snow from the driveways and paths was refreshing, and provided a physical outlet for the sexual frustration that still clung to him. He felt much better after a few hours of hard work, until he let himself think about the kiss from the night before, and the soft bedsheets that Lydia was sleeping on. How the pink roses that covered the bed would provide such a stark contrast to the inked flowers and designs on her skin.

Suddenly, he was much warmer than he should be, not even feeling the wind as it passed by.

Down, boy. She wasn't interested.

She'd kissed him like she was interested, another part of him argued. He could press the issue, and she might give in—and then what? She'd be pissed at him again. And rightfully so.

Chemistry was only hormones, after all, and he was a Marine, right? Self-control was hardwired into his way of life. And when this was done, he'd go back to the Caribbean and help himself to any one—or maybe more—of the beautiful women there who were always available. He stood, taking a breath as he shoveled a path to the front door of the farmhouse, refocusing.

Clearing the final bit of snow in front of the steps, he looked across the field where Lydia expertly managed the tractor, clearing the area around the garage so that she could get her car out. Who would have known?

She constantly surprised him. He wished he could take a picture of her on his phone and send it to Tessa— she was certain to be as surprised by this other side of Lydia as he was.

If Lydia ever told her. Hopefully, she would. Tessa was made of strong stuff, and she stood by her friends. Lydia had to trust in that.

Planting his shovel in the snow, he saw that Smitty and Kyle had gone to take care of the animals, and Lydia was still pushing snow around with the tractor. Ely decided to take the opportunity to look around while everyone else was occupied. He'd already noticed that none of the locks or windows had been broken or jimmied. Lydia had locked her doors, so how had the intruder gained entry?

It was an old door, old lock, and it was possible Lydia's mother had handed out copies of the keys to anyone she thought needed one. He'd have to find out. He planned to buy new locks and install them first thing, and seek out the local sheriff and talk to him about what was going on. Just in case.

He'd promised Lydia he wouldn't tell Tessa, but he'd never said he wouldn't tell the local authorities what had happened.

Wandering around the outside of the house, predictably, any footsteps were erased by snow, but he saw something small and off-color kick up through the snow as he stepped and bent to retrieve a small vial. It was empty, and it could be anything. Still, he put it in his pocket.

As he turned the corner toward the back, he was interrupted.

"Looking for something?"

Kyle was standing by the edge of the porch, watching him closely. How did this guy keep managing to get the drop on him?

"Thought I dropped my keys, but I guess I left them inside," Ely lied smoothly.

Smitty was a good enough guy, but Kyle gave him an itchy feeling. He was protective of Lydia, but there was something shifty about him, as well. Kyle watched more than he talked, and he watched Lydia in particular. Ely didn't like it.

Kyle barked out a short laugh. "If you lost them out here, you're sunk. And wouldn't that be convenient? Give you another excuse to stay."

Ely smiled, but there was no humor in it. "Turns out I don't need an excuse. I'll be staying awhile. I'm going to help out a bit while I'm here."

Kyle didn't seem to like that idea very much, but just shrugged. "Whatever," Kyle said with a snort, and turned to walk away, heading back to the barn.

Maybe a background check into Kyle wouldn't be a bad idea, Ely thought as he went inside to get his keys— where he had left them on the counter just inside the door. Beside them, he saw a slip of paper and picked it up. It was a veterinary report on one of the cows—the animal had been poisoned.

The door opened and closed behind him, and he turned to find Lydia, pink-cheeked from her outdoor exertions. Their eyes met and held for a second, before she walked past.

"What happened to this cow?" he asked, the piece of paper still in his hand.

Her eyes darkened. "Well, if you read it, you already know. But it's fine. We got to it in time."

He touched her elbow as she passed him. "Lydia, someone tried to kill one of your animals—and Kyle told me about the spray paint."

She took a breath. "Listen, there are some people from my past who might not be crazy about me coming back. I think as soon as they know I'm not staying, this will stop."

"What else?"

Reluctantly, she told him.

"And the sheriff wouldn't help?"

"There was nothing they could do. It's not exactly a situation for them to send out a forensics team and post surveillance," she said sarcastically, but he sensed the agitation, and the fear, underneath her tone.

"Okay, well, hopefully my presence here in the house might discourage anyone, as well."

She agreed.

He paused, inhaling. The house smelled amazing and his mouth watered. He hadn't eaten anything since the night before, and his stomach was reminding him now. Loudly.

"What smells so good?"

"I made a batch of pancakes earlier and left them warming in the oven before I went outside. Let me get the coffee on, and the eggs and sausage, and we can all have brunch in about an hour."

"All?"

"Yeah. My mother always had everyone in for Sunday breakfast, but Thursday works, too, considering how hard everyone is going at it out there," she said, peeling off her coat and gloves—much sturdier winter gear than she had been wearing the night before—to reveal her slim, petite figure.

"What can I do to help?" Ely offered.

He suspected maybe that she wanted to invite the ranch hands in so that they weren't here alone together. Probably a good idea until he got the hang of this being friends thing.

"I've got it covered. I think Kyle was going to try to get the tractor over to dig out your truck. You should probably go help him with that. If it keeps snowing like this, we're going to have to unbury everything again by dinner. You'll want to get your truck in the garage and under cover."

"Thanks. If I can get out today, I need to go settle up on my room and get my things. I'll stop by the hardware store to pick up some supplies, as well."

Lydia turned to pull some pans out of a cupboard, and the movement drew his eyes to the curve of her backside, and as her shirt rode up, to the scroll of ink that was sketched across her lower back.

"You can take my—well, it was my mother's—car if you need to. It's all-wheel drive and should get around okay."

"Thanks," he said, turning away as she bent deep into a cupboard, her butt poking up in a very delectable way, making him think thoughts that he wasn't supposed to be thinking.

After all, they were only friends. Repeating that to himself a couple of hundred times as he went to get Kyle, he hoped it would eventually sink in.

IT TURNED OUT THAT Ely would have been stuck there whether Lydia had agreed to let him stay or not. They were well and truly snowed in from the storm the night before, and they hadn't been able to get anywhere close to Ely's truck. The highway plows had come by and pretty much buried it—they'd have to try again tomorrow, when the snow stopped. If the snow stopped.

Lydia kept herself from obsessing about Ely's presence by making enough pancakes, sausage and home fries for an army. She couldn't get his offer out of her mind—some frisky fun while they were stuck here together, no expectations, no strings attached.

Normally, she would have jumped at such an offer. So why wasn't she? Ely was hot, and he was wonderful in bed. No doubt he could offer her some much-needed distraction from her other, less pleasant tasks. And if she was completely honest, it felt good to have him around, and that he knew about the stuff that had been going on.

She went back to cooking, hearing their footsteps on the porch. She walked back to open the door she had locked behind her. Lydia stood in the doorway for a moment, looking at a world turned completely white, as the men entered the kitchen.

"I'd forgotten what winter here is like," she said to no one, but found Ely was right behind her. Of course he was, she thought with a sigh. She'd felt him watching her earlier, knew he was fascinated with her ink from the night they'd shared. "It really is like living in a snow globe."

"We have our share of storms back east, but yeah. This is pretty amazing," Ely said as he looked with her out at snow that piled over the porch rails, glittering everywhere.

"And it's just the beginning of the season," she added. Then, catching a chill when the wind whipped toward them, she stepped back to close the door, bumping solidly into him.

His hands landed on her waist, steadying her. His thumb slid along the waist of her jeans, grazing her skin at the small of her back and she stilled. He stepped away without another word, but the heat that leaped between them from the simple touch seemed to brand her.

Neither Smitty nor Kyle had seemed to notice anything. As the men ate, Lydia dug out some of her father's winter clothes for Ely, since the ones he'd worn that morning were soaked. Breakfast passed uneventfully, and they went back to work outside, while she stayed indoors and worked on clearing out some more of her mother's things.

As the men talked over coffee during an afternoon break, Lydia slipped away upstairs to take a shower and change. She was exhausted, not having slept much the night before, and she closed her eyes under the hot water of the shower only to shriek a few seconds later as it suddenly turned ice cold.

She jumped again as the bathroom door burst open and Ely was there, looking fierce, facing her as she wrapped the shower curtain around herself.

"Ely! What are you doing? Get out!" she demanded, her teeth chattering.

"You screamed. What's wrong?"

She closed her eyes, understanding why he would be in bodyguard mode after the events of the previous evening. She sighed, praying for patience.

"I didn't scream, I yelled. In surprise. Cold water. The water heater must have broken."

His body eased, the tension draining out of him as he realized she wasn't in trouble, but his gaze didn't leave her.

"I'll let Smitty know," he said distractedly, his eyes glued to her. The transparent plastic of the curtain wasn't hiding much.

"Thanks," she said, swallowing hard as she confronted the desire in his eyes.

"Um, could you hand me one of those towels?"

He blinked, as if breaking out of a trance, and grabbed a fluffy white towel from the counter, handing it to her. This time, when their fingers brushed, they both pulled back as if electricity sparked between them.

"You have to go," Lydia said, fighting the wave of desire that had hit as soon as he walked through the door. She only wanted him to get undressed and join her. "The guys are going to wonder—"

"Ely? Everything okay up there?" Smitty's shout interrupted them, yanking them out of their daze.

"Yeah, Smitty. Everything's okay. Apparently the hot water heater broke," Ely said, tearing his gaze away from hers and walking back out the door, closing it firmly behind him.

Lydia let go of the breath she was holding and wrapped the towel around herself, stepping out and sinking down to sit on the side of the tub.

Why did she have to feel this way about Tessa's brother-in-law, for crying out loud?

The night they'd met, he'd told her about the woman who had dumped him, and about the life he'd thought they could have until he found out she wasn't so perfect after all.

Chloe Roberts, an up-and-coming investigative reporter with a father who was highly placed in the U.S. Navy had been the woman to send Ely into a tailspin. And had shot him directly into Lydia's path. Chloe was supermodel-gorgeous, smart, sophisticated and she'd had Ely wrapped around her little finger—except that she was also wearing an engagement ring on that finger—given to her by another man.

Ely hadn't known, and he was crushed, not only by losing his dreams, but by unknowingly having slept with a woman who belonged to someone else. Lydia knew he never would have done that if he had known; Chloe had played him for a fool.

Lydia had taken him back to her place because she wanted to ease some of his pain. It wasn't an instinct she'd often given in to, nor one she had very often; normally, sex was simply entertainment for her. But Ely had been different.

It made perfect sense that he'd used her to forget Chloe, at least for a night—Lydia was the exact opposite of the reporter. For the short while he'd been with her, she had made sure that he wouldn't think about what he'd lost. Problem was, Lydia hadn't been able to forget him.

Maybe she was thinking about this the wrong way. By avoiding sex, they were making it a bigger deal than it was. The sexual tension was driving them crazy. Lydia was friends with several of her former lovers, and she knew that desire always seemed to burn out naturally after a while, leaving friendship in its wake. Why wouldn't it be the same with Ely?

Lydia was no Chloe Roberts, and she wasn't thirteen anymore, either. But Ely wanted her, and why did it have to be so complicated? She had the things she wanted in life: her business, her friends. Those were the things that counted, and she was lucky to have them. There was a time in her life when she didn't think she deserved even that much.

Making her way to her room, she took a breath and

toweled off, trying to warm up as she dressed and checked out the window, finding Ely with Smitty, moving hay to the barn. Though he was bundled in the thick, wool coat of her father's, she could see how strong he was just by the easy way he lifted the block of hay and the grace of his movements. As if the heavy bundles of hay weighed nothing.

He was like that in bed, too. Even when he was pushed to the limit, every muscle tensed in high relief as she brought him to the edge over and over, he was the most perfect man she'd ever seen. Certainly the most perfect man she'd ever been with.

It had been such a thrill to have such a powerful man give himself over that way and to watch the intense pleasure he experienced. With her.

Or had he been thinking of Chloe all along? Was Lydia that foolish? Frowning, she supposed it was possible. He had just broken up with the woman less than a day before. He admitted that he hadn't been thinking straight at the time.

She shook her head in disgust, walking away from the window. It hadn't even been twenty-four hours and she was already trying to find ways to renege on their agreement. She recited to herself, again, all of the reasons this couldn't happen. But in her heart, she would be amazed if either of them lasted the week.

5

LATER THAT AFTERNOON, when they had finally finished clearing the snow, Lydia couldn't help but notice that Ely looked like he was having the best time of his life.

"I think I have time to get into town. Still mind if I borrow your keys?" he asked.

"Actually, would it be okay if I go into town with you? I need to pick up some supplies."

"No problem. I'll heat up the car."

She handed him her keys and their fingers touched without them bursting into spontaneous flames. See, they could be friends, right? They just had to get through this awkward stage. The moment in the shower had just been…well, a moment.

It didn't mean anything she didn't want it to mean.

Once they got to town, they went their separate ways. And Lydia tried to focus on what she needed to buy for the ranch.

She walked to the small grocery store, figuring she would start there. But as she made her way down the aisles, feeling again like she was out of place, worried that she would bump into someone who would know her, she forgot the list in her hand and found herself staring at a display, lost in another one of the time warps she seemed to be suffering since she'd returned to Clear River. She even heard someone saying her name.

"Lydia Hamilton," the guy said again, and she turned around slowly, grabbing one package of paper towels from the shelf and tossing them in the basket. She didn't look up, facing him, though the second time he'd spoken, she recognized his voice.

"Loyal," she said with a quick stretch of her mouth that didn't quite approach a smile. "Long time."

Loyal Slater. Football star, high-school hunk, and her first kiss in their freshman year of high school. His parents owned the ranch bordering her family's land. That kiss had been the beginning and end of their relationship, since Loyal was anything but.

"We heard you went off and became a big-city girl," he said. "Sorry about your mom, by the way."

"Thanks," she said with a nod, anxious to finish her shopping and leave.

She hated coming into town like this. The fewer people she ran into in the process, the better. Strolls down memory lane with old boyfriends were a case in point.

Loyal was all grown up and still as handsome as ever. He kept staring at her piercings like he hadn't seen anything like them before, but she'd passed two tat shops in Billings, and knew that Montana wasn't that removed from the ways of the world.

Still, her winter clothes covered the majority of her designs, which often drew attention even back in the city. Lydia considered it good advertising. When people asked her about her ink, she often talked them into visiting her shop, and she had found a lot of customers that way.

"Hey, listen, if you need any help with anything at the house, let us know," Loyal offered. "Old times and all," he added awkwardly as she stared at him, silent, unsure what to say.

"Thanks, but I'm good," she settled on, starting to turn away.

"Merry Christmas, anyway," he said.

"Yeah, uh, you, too," she mumbled, anxious to get back to her list, but as she turned the corner of the aisle, Lydia felt as if she were caught in *A Christmas Carol*, facing the ghost of Christmas past.

"Ginny," she said on a sharp intake of breath, facing the one person she had hoped to avoid.

"Lydia," the woman in the wheelchair, facing her in front of the display of Christmas candy, said, looking apprehensive and just as surprised as Lydia was.

"I heard you were back," Ginny said.

Lydia felt as if her throat was closing, and all she wanted to do was throw her basket and run, but she managed to nod.

"I need to take care of Mom's place," she said stiffly, looking away, her eyes landing on the Christmas candy but not really seeing it.

"You're selling?"

"Um, yeah," she said, looking back at the rubber tires of the chair, and Ginny's pink boots, planted on the foot holders. Ginny had always loved everything pink. Lydia had once, too.

"I, um," Lydia stuttered, looking for words, and saw the ice slide over her former friend's gaze as someone else walked up to join them. A man unloaded some things into a cart, and shifted to face Ginny with a smile.

"I think that's it, darlin'," he said affectionately, and then turned a smile in Lydia's direction. "Hi, there."

Lydia nodded, taking in the guy's handsome face, and his business-casual dress. A wool coat, nice leather boots. A businessman, not a ranch worker.

"And you are?" he asked.

"This is Lydia Hamilton, my best friend from high school," Ginny said bitterly, her eyes pinning Lydia to the spot. "Lydia, this is my husband, Charles."

Husband. Lydia had known that, her mother had told her that Ginny had gotten married somewhere along the line. But she remained speechless.

"Why are you bothering my wife?" her husband asked, his smile fading. "Why are you even here? You leave us alone," he warned darkly, sending Lydia another look as he put a hand on Ginny's shoulder.

Lydia opened her mouth to say something, but nothing came out. She met Ginny's eyes, wishing there was something that could be said, but clearly her friend didn't want to hear any of it, and Lydia couldn't blame her. The resentment and accusation in her eyes and tone were all that Lydia could expect.

"Take care of yourself, Lydia. It is what you do best," Ginny said coldly, spinning her chair and following her husband to the register.

Lydia's knees were shaking, and it was all she could do to stand up. Abandoning her basket of items, she made her way to the door and out, needing air. Needing to escape.

Her mother had told her she should confront her past. That Ginny had moved on with her life—which was clear—and that Lydia needed to make peace with it, too. But that was clearly impossible.

Lydia knew her mother was wrong; she didn't expect forgiveness. It wasn't even possible. She deserved their rebuff, and worse. She had been wrong to avoid them, however. Maybe allowing them to say what they'd said was only fair. She'd never given Ginny that chance before.

Everyone thought Lydia was so cool, so brave. She was the most cowardly person she knew, she thought miserably. Leaning into the car, her face fell into her hands, the cold air helping her to settle down a bit.

"Hey, what's going on—are you okay?"

Lydia jumped at the sound of Ely's voice. In her shock and upset, she had completely forgotten about him.

"Um, I just have a really bad headache," she said.

"You're white as a sheet. Get in the car," he said, opening the door and ushering her in before he went around to the other side to climb in. He turned the heat on full blast and took her freezing hands between his, warming him.

"Are you sick? Or did something else happen?" he asked, his gaze severe and concerned all at once.

Lydia couldn't talk about it, least of all with him. What would Ely think, or Tessa, or anyone, if they knew what she'd done? Maybe they deserved to know, too, but she couldn't do it. Not now.

"The headache just got to me. That's all," she hedged, and could see in his face that he wasn't buying it, but he nodded.

"Okay. Did you get your groceries?"

"No." Her eyes burned and she cursed, not wanting to cry in front of anyone, especially Ely. Biting down, she swallowed hard, and took a breath, straightening her spine. Looking up, she watched as Ginny and her husband left the store and made their way to their truck.

"This store didn't have what we needed," she fibbed. "Maybe if we try the one in Billings? They have the larger places to shop."

Ely nodded. "Sure. We can do that, but are you sure you feel well enough?"

"I'm fine. Really. Just tired, and a headache, but I'll be okay. Let's go?" she said, anxious to escape.

Nodding, he put the car in gear and pulled away from the curb. Lydia focused out the window, getting a hold on herself, trying to focus away from the nauseous feeling that hadn't quite passed. She was running away again, and she knew it. But what did confronting anything do—it just made everyone unhappy.

She would see Ginny's unhappy face in front of her for the rest of her life, and maybe that was as it should be. The only solution was to wrap things up here and leave as soon as she could, after Christmas, as her mother's will provided. Then she could go back home and try to bury it all in the past, for good.

ELY WAS ABLE TO get his truck out of the snowbank the next day, and was in the sheriff's office, waiting to see the man himself. It was the one thing he was unable to do the day before when Lydia had come into town with him, though he still hadn't been able to get that out of his mind.

On the way to the city and back, she had been quiet, pale, and not entirely like herself. He knew it was more than a simple headache that had set her off. When he'd found her by the car, she had been shattered—he had actually been afraid for her until she seemed to calm down.

She didn't say another word about it during their entire drive and had gone to bed after they finished putting away the supplies. Ely had a feeling she had a scare of some sort, and he wasn't going to just sit by and do nothing.

A group of sullen teenage boys slouched on the bench in the corner, looking like they didn't care about anything, but their clenched fingers, tapping feet and sidelong glances betrayed their worry. Ely caught the eye of one who looked like the youngest of the four and leaned forward.

"What ya in for?" he said with a conspiratorial wink.

The kid started to say something when the older boy next to him elbowed him in the ribs.

"Shut up, doofus. He's trying to get you to confess."

Ely's eyebrows rose. "Confess? Nah, I'm just making conversation," he said.

The older boy snorted in disbelief, crossing his arms over his middle.

"But if I had to guess," Ely continued. "I'd say you were caught—during school hours—smoking something down behind someone's barn, yeah?" They reeked of pot, whether they realized it or not.

"We weren't behind a barn, we were—"

Another elbow to the ribs got the two boys into a small scuffle, and Ely had to hide a smile. They thought they were so tough.

The door to Sheriff Granger's office opened, and he emerged, walking over to the boys. They didn't quite meet his eyes as he towered over them, a big man, not too much older than Ely.

"I just got off the phone with each of your parents. They'll be down to get you soon, and in exchange for not charging you and locking you up for the weekend, they agreed that you all should spend the next week cleaning out Mr. Mason's barn."

All four heads snapped up. "Are you kidding?" the older one said. "That place is a dump. It'll take forever."

"That's right. Added to that, you'll be in school, and I'll be making spot phone calls to make sure you are. If any of you do this again, you won't get a second chance, got it? I'll put you in the tank, and if we don't have room for you here, since it can get a little crowded over Christmas, we'll send you over to Powell, you got it?"

"You can't do that," the belligerent older boy asserted, standing. "We're minors, and it was just some weed," he said, and then frowned as he realized what he'd just confessed aloud.

"Good going, Rog," the kid next to him taunted.

The sheriff leaned in close. "You want to make a bet on what I can do, Roger? Push your luck, and you'll see how far I'm willing to go to make sure you aren't bringing that kind of trouble into this town, to these kids," the sheriff said in his best Dirty Harry–type voice, which Ely thought he pulled off pretty well.

The boy sneered, but backed down, sitting back on the bench.

"Yeah, shut up, Rog, before you get us into more trouble," the younger one said, earning a punch in the arm.

"Cut it out," Sheriff Granger barked, and the boys went quiet and still. "You'll report to Mr. Mason directly after school. I'll have a deputy stop by and make sure you're there. Your parents will pick you up when you're done and bring you home. Got it? You won't be finished with the job until I go to inspect that barn and say you're done."

The boys nodded glumly.

"Think about it the next time you decide to skip school to do something illegal," the sheriff said. He proceeded to tell the receptionist something and then turned to Ely.

"Can I help you? Stella says you've been waiting to see me?"

Ely stood, put his hand out. "I'd appreciate a few minutes, if you have the time."

"Sure. Now that I've got the Wild Bunch here all settled," he said, sliding a look at the boys again as he led Ely into his office.

"My brothers and I got into trouble quite a bit at about that age, too. Never drugs, but other stuff we were too stupid to avoid. Compared to what our father made us do, those guys got off easy."

Sheriff Granger laughed. "I don't know about that. Hank Mason is kind of the town eccentric—one of those TV shows might call him a hoarder of sorts. That barn is a fire hazard. Hank finally agreed to have it cleaned out, so this works out well on all sides. I don't even want to think about the crap those kids are going to have to dig through," the sheriff said with a grin. "I should probably get them hazmat suits."

Ely laughed. "I bet they'll learn their lesson, then."

"The young ones, yeah. The older one, Roger, he's had some problems since his parents split up. He's heading down a bad path, and we're just trying to keep him from taking his younger friends down with him."

Ely nodded. "Nice thing about a town like this is that you can give them that kind of attention."

There were so many kids in the city that went unnoticed, and ended up lost for good. Jonas had been a cop for several years, and some of the stories he told from those days painted a sad, dark picture of the inner city.

"Don't kid yourself. We try, but the problems get more serious here all the time. Meth labs, illegals, domestic violence. It's a small town, but we have the same challenges some of the cities have, and fewer people to cover them. Anyway…you are?"

"Ely Berringer. I'm in town for a few days, visiting a friend. Lydia Hamilton."

"Right. I heard Lydia was back in town, but our paths haven't crossed yet."

"You know her?"

"She was friends with my younger sister Ginny when we were growing up. Always wondered what happened to her after she took off. Sorry to hear about her mama, though," the sheriff offered. "Faye was a great lady. A cornerstone of the town."

Ely recognized the name, Ginny, from the yearbook he'd seen. "Lydia has been having some trouble since she's come back to town. She didn't want to make a fuss over it—she seems to think it's nothing, but I'm concerned."

The sheriff's eyes narrowed as he sat back in his chair.

"What kind of trouble, exactly?"

"Small stuff around the ranch, so I've heard—messages left, broken fences. Two guys were harassing her at the bar night before last. But later that same night, someone was in her house. Luckily, she had a gun, and one of her ranch hands and I were close by. Drove the guy off."

The sheriff straightened, grabbed a pen. "An intruder? Why didn't she call us?"

"She did. Your deputy told her there wasn't anything they could do, and so she didn't see the point in calling back."

The men took each other in for a few seconds, sizing each other up.

"I wasn't informed. She must not have filed a formal report, or I would have seen it. Was she hurt?" Granger asked.

Ely shook his head. "They vandalized her kitchen, broke some stuff. It shook her up. I found this in the snow by the house the next day," he said, taking the vial out of his pocket.

Granger scrutinized it in his hand. "This could be anything."

"It looks like vials I've seen used for drugs."

Granger's eyebrows shot up. "You have a lot of experience in that area?"

"I've seen my share when I was in Afghanistan, and on the streets. My brother was a cop for a while."

"The house has been empty and sometimes folks will scan the obits looking for places to loot. As for this, I can try it for prints and contents, but I wouldn't expect much. It could have been on the ground for who knows how long," the sheriff countered.

"I don't think it was kids or thieves in the house. They didn't take anything, and why not do it before the house was occupied? Lydia said someone here might be bearing some sort of grudge, and if so, how far they might be willing to go to deliver that message."

"Lydia tell you that? That someone has a grudge?"

"Just my gut."

"You're in law enforcement?" the sheriff asked.

"I was in the Marines, and I work as private security with a firm back in Philly. I came out here to check on Lydia, as a friend."

"So you were the guy who phoned in the complaint about the two guys harassing a woman last night near Hailey's?"

Ely nodded. "Saw it all myself if you need a witness."

"I took care of it," Granger said succinctly, clearly closing off that thread in their discussion. "Lydia left a long time ago—under bad circumstances, that was true—but I don't think anyone would hold that against her now."

"What bad circumstances?" Ely asked, noting that the sheriff had completely ignored his question about the two cowboys.

Granger grimaced. "Water under the bridge. It's up to her to tell you, if she wants to. I can go by the house, talk to her, get a statement and look around the place. Other than that, there's not a lot I can do."

Ely frowned. Lydia wouldn't be happy if Granger came by, and even more so if she knew Ely had sent him in her direction.

"I don't think she'll tell you anything more than she told me. I just wanted you to have a head's-up, in case anything else happens. Or in case there's anything I should know, maybe."

Granger stood. "Okay, then."

Wow, closed book, Ely thought.

"Do you know the guy who works on the ranch? Kyle?"

"Kyle Jones? I don't know much. He's worked the ranch for a little less than a year, keeps to himself. Never gave me any reason to deal with him," Sheriff Granger said with a shrug.

Ely stood, knowing when not to push the issue. "Well, then, thank you for your time."

"Happy to oblige," Granger said, shaking his hand and picking up the phone as Ely went out the door. "Let me know if there's anything else I can do."

The sheriff was a nice enough guy, but Ely thought he wasn't being completely forthright, and he'd detected some sort of change in his demeanor when Granger spoke about Lydia's past. Taking out his cell as he got into the truck and turned the heat on, he waited until his brother Jonas picked up on the other end.

"Ely? What's up?" Jonas asked, sounding distracted.

"You got a minute?"

"Just. Have the FBI on the other line."

"Listen, when you get a chance, can you do a background check on a guy named Kyle Jones, probably in his late thirties. Drives a Ford Ranger, here's the license number," Ely said, rattling it off.

"Looking for anything in particular?"

"Anything…off. Criminal record, that kind of thing. Maybe his job and bank records. Also…" Ely paused, wondering if he really wanted to have Jonas look into Ginny Granger's past. And Lydia's.

"What?"

"Never mind," he said, not wanting to go there, not yet.

"Okay, I gotta go. I'll let you know what I find."

"Thanks."

They hung up, and Ely pulled out of the space and scanned the dark clouds hanging to the north. They were a ways off, and he was hungry. For more than dinner, he realized with a frown, Lydia's soft scent haunting him. Whatever was happening, he wasn't going anywhere until she left, and he knew she was safe. For that reason and others, he was looking forward to getting back to the ranch, maybe more than he should be.

6

LYDIA WAS SITTING in the middle of about one million items she'd pulled out of the downstairs drawers, closets and storage areas, where she had been working since that afternoon. She was hoping to sort through it all for what she wanted to keep—very little—and what would go to Goodwill or be thrown out. It was impossible. So many things just needed to go, but she felt guilty getting rid of them. It was like throwing her family history away.

The worst part of it had been finding a stash of Christmas gifts—for her, wrapped and hidden away in the closet. Her mom mailed Lydia gifts every year. Although Lydia always told her it wasn't necessary. She must have wrapped these just before she'd gotten sick.

That had done Lydia in, bringing on waves of tears that wrung her out. So here she sat, surrounded by the guts of several storage closets and cheerfully wrapped presents, feeling wretched.

Scanning the room, she was overwhelmed—again—and quite sure she could never do this. She should have never come back here, but it was too late now. Emotionally overloaded and exhausted, which seemed to be her constant state lately, she stood, trying to shake off her blues. She needed to do something positive. Something reenergizing.

Something wild.

Lydia wanted to feel like herself again and not the version of herself that she'd been since arriving back at the ranch. She'd been depressed, overemotional and moody—which she supposed was natural, given the situation—but she needed a break from herself. A break from everything.

There was one thing—one person—who could make her forget it all. Just for a while.

Suddenly, seducing Ely was such an obvious thing to do that she wondered why she had been so conflicted about it in the first place. Back home, she wouldn't have thought twice; she would have slept with him until one of them was bored and moved on.

The only reason she'd been reading more into what she'd had with him was because she'd been on the fritz for the last few months emotionally—her mother's illness, Tessa's wedding—it had all fried her circuits. She hadn't been thinking straight. This moment seemed like the first crystal clear one she'd had in weeks.

Once decided, the need to be with him turned almost desperate. She abandoned her work to head upstairs, stripping as she went. She was covered in dust, sweaty from removing snow and digging out old closets, so her first stop was the shower. She just hoped there was time to get ready before he came home from his errands. He'd been making plans for fix-it projects all morning, and then out finding hardware supplies the rest of the day, from what she knew.

Noting the time, she realized she hadn't even thought

about dinner—breakfast had been huge again, as she fed the guys as they continued to work outside—and she still had leftovers in the fridge.

But food was the last of her concerns. Other appetites were calling her right now.

A smile formed, feline and anticipatory. She didn't have any of her really fun toys here—she hadn't expected to need them—but she could improvise. Out of the shower, Lydia ran her hands over arms, unsure if her goose bumps were from the slight chill of the upstairs or from the different ways she could imagine to seduce Ely. What was the most creative way to let him know she had changed her mind about their arrangement?

She could wait downstairs on the sofa, naked. That would get to the point with minimal fuss. Or, she could leave him little notes all through the house, leading him where she wanted him to go. She could take some snapshots of herself in sexy poses and leave them scattered in a path he would follow to her bedroom door.

Maybe send a digital image to his phone? No, that was dangerous—she never let compromising pictures of herself online anywhere. While she enjoyed an adventurous sex life, the last thing she needed was a nude photo of her ending up on YouTube or wherever.

Searching through her clothes, she hadn't brought a whole lot of anything sexy with her, either. As she picked up a bottle of spicy-scented skin lotion Tessa had made just for her—Lydia's own original scent—she heard the crunch of tires on the driveway, which signaled Ely's return. She growled in frustration at her lack of timing. Maybe she should wait....

No, then she'd lose her nerve or let her head take over again. This was about *not* thinking.

Walking to the window, she looked down and saw

Ely emerging from the garage, his arms packed with bags and a duffel thrown over his back. It was all the inspiration she needed, as she tapped lightly on the cold window. Then again, harder.

He paused, detecting the sound, and looked up.

Following her instincts, she dropped the towel, but left the sheer curtains drawn. It would create a little mystery.

He looked around, as if checking to see if anyone was there—she froze, too, not even thinking that she might be giving a show for more than one.

But then he turned to face the window squarely, his eyes seeming to stare right into hers, even through the curtain.

Slowly lifting her leg, she planted her toes on the bottom windowsill, a shiver running through her. She reached to get some more of her lotion, bending forward to work it up her leg, over her thigh. She didn't look at him, but paid attention to her ministrations, as if she had no idea someone was watching. One leg done, she did the other, and then moved her hands up over her lower stomach, her waist and her arms.

Peeking out the window, she saw that he was still there. Watching, waiting.

She poured out a little more lotion and let her head fall back as she applied it to her neck and throat, and then finally to her breasts, lingering there, playing with her nipples. They were already hard from knowing he was watching. She gasped at the sweet sensations, enjoying touching herself for Ely's pleasure. And hers. Her breath came faster as she warmed up more. When she looked down again, he was gone.

The slam of a door.

Something was dropped.

Heavy boot steps on the stairs.

The next thing she knew, he was there, standing in the doorway of her bedroom. His eyes were hot, watching her, hunger etched into every contour of his face.

"Finish," was all he said.

She faced him, met his gaze with her own and continued to stroke one breast as her other hand moved lower, down between her thighs.

She was wet, swollen, and she moaned as her fingers moved lightly over her sensitive flesh.

"Turn and put your leg up on the chair, so I can see," he ordered, his own breath short as he took off his jacket.

It thrilled her, how he gave orders. She did as she was told, placing her foot up on the chair by the vanity, letting her knee fall to the side so that he could see. Her fingers slipped back, pressing inside as she used the heel of her hand to massage her clit. As she sped closer to completion, her head fell forward, her body giving itself up to the intensity of her touch, his gaze.

"Come, Lydia," he said roughly, and she did, almost on his command, crying out as her hips bucked and the orgasm made her knees weak, threatening the stability of her stance.

No worries though, as Ely was there, behind her, his hands on her waist. He held her as the pleasure faded and her mind cleared.

Lydia met his eyes in the mirror. It was good, but it wasn't enough. She wanted him, and clearly he was feeling the same way.

"Why did you change your mind?" he asked against her ear.

She shook her head. "No talking, no thinking…just this," she said softly, taking his hands and placing them over her breasts, pressing her butt back against the ridge along the front of his jeans.

Ely didn't have to be told twice, removing his hands in order to shuck his own clothes. Then he was there, hot and hard behind her.

"Yes, like that," Lydia moaned as the heat of his body pressed into hers, lowering her leg so that she had both feet on the floor. She bent over the vanity, wanting him now. She was even hotter, primed for him.

"Just a second," he said gruffly, leaving the room.

She wanted to object, to not let any crack of daylight drive away the haze of need that consumed her, but she knew what he had left for, and kept herself hot by touching herself again while he was gone. Back in less than a minute, he stood in the doorway and cursed softly, apparently liking what he saw.

She vaguely heard the sound of a packet ripping, and a moment later he was behind her, his hands coming around to her breasts. Lydia supported herself with one hand on the vanity as her fingers caressed the sensitive spot between her legs. His mouth was on her back, her neck, kissing, licking and nibbling her all over, leaving bliss in its wake.

She lifted her hips, reached back, took him in her hand and brought him to where she most wanted him. He didn't press forward, still kissing, teasing and driving her crazy.

"Please, Ely," she panted. Even the tip of his cock felt broad and heavy against her, and she wanted all of him. Wanted him to fill her and obliterate anything else from her consciousness.

"I like it when you beg," he said with a light chuckle, pushing inside a little, then pulling back, making her whimper. His hands tweaked her nipples and then moved to her hips, holding her steady. "Look up, Lydia."

Lifting up and planting both hands on the dresser, she met his eyes in the mirror that hung in back of the vanity. The vision she found there was almost enough to make her climax, but not quite—he was her fantasy. A hot, powerful, hungry male animal, bending her over, taking what he wanted.

"Don't look away," he said, his jaw clenched tight as he held her firmly, sliding inside in one deep thrust that went so deep she gasped, every thick inch of him buried in her. Her fingers clawed the edge of the vanity, but she didn't look away. Wiggling her hips a little, she was impatient, wanting more.

A light swat on her backside made her gasp—her eyes widening in delighted surprise.

Ely shook his head at her in the mirror, looking severe in a very sexy way. "Don't move unless I tell you."

His demands made her hotter than she would have thought, and she nodded, making herself stay still. He did, too, remaining still and deep inside. His hands soothed over her back, her butt, everywhere, until she moaned from the sweet intensity of it, the pressure that made her need so much more. It was so, so hard not to move against him, but she didn't—she wanted to do whatever he told her, giving control over to him completely.

It was wonderful.

He slipped one arm under her lower stomach, lifting her up a little more as his other hand cupped her breast. Finally, incredibly, he began to move.

Lydia thought she might pass out from the sheer relief and sharp pleasure that came from the friction of his withdrawl, but when he thrust forward again, harder this time, she cursed from the strength of her response. Ely smiled at her in the reflection, and she smiled back.

Nothing else existed now, nothing but the two of them trapped in this moment, caught in their reflected image in the mirror and in each other's eyes. He found a rhythm that became her world. It wasn't long before his moans mingled with her cries, his fingers gripping her backside tightly as he lost himself and she followed him, again. They never stopped looking at each other, not even as their world dwindled down to spent gasps and weak-limbed pleasure.

"Damn, Lydia," he managed, gulping hard breaths, his magnificent body covered in a sheen of perspiration. He was like a work of art, or, in her eyes, the perfect canvas.

He lifted her up and held her against him. They stood in silence like that, wrapped around each other until their breathing eased. Ely took her hand, leading her back down to the shower where they stepped in and rinsed off. Lydia smiled against his shoulder as he ran the soap over her.

"What's funny?"

"This is my second shower in one evening," she said, grinning.

"I can probably make it more fun," he said, moving the sponge in his hands down between her thighs.

"Oh, I bet you can," she said, laughing and wiggling away. "But let's save some for later."

His hands came up, wound to her hair and she was caught off guard when he kissed her so deeply that it stole any thoughts she might have had for several long minutes. He was semi-erect against her thigh.

"I don't think that will be a problem" he said, nudging her and shutting off the water. "But I did pick up some takeout for dinner. It's probably cold, but I figured I would bring something home since you've been cooking these large breakfasts for all of us."

"That was nice of you, but where did you get takeout around here?"

"I drove into Billings and got some Thai."

She looked at him in amazement as they stepped out and took towels from the rack.

"You drove all the way into the city for takeout?"

"The roads were pretty clear, and I made it back before the storm started again. I guess you could say I had a bad craving."

"Yeah, me, too," she said with a wicked smile, though she didn't mean the food, though that was good, too. She was starving. This was exactly what she needed. This was how life was supposed to feel. Good, hot and easy.

"Thanks for doing that. We can heat it up."

They changed into some clothes and went downstairs. Lydia smiled a little when she spotted the pile of packages and his green duffel bag all dropped right inside the door.

"In a hurry, were you?"

"You could say that. I almost had a heart attack when I saw you in that window. I, um…" he started to say something, and then seemed to hold back as he picked up some of the packages from the floor, throwing his duffel over near the stairs.

"What?"

He looked at her with so much heat, she thought her bones might melt.

"The other night, when I was walking up from where my truck went off the road, I saw you then, too. Undressing by the window. You nearly drove me out of my mind. This was like a private fantasy coming true," he said, his voice lowering, reflecting the desire that sparked in his eyes.

Lydia had no idea he had been watching her, and the idea turned her on.

"We'd better stop talking about this and heat up dinner, or we'll starve to death," she said, loving how the sheer power of sex had warmed her, made her blood pound and her spirit feel lighter. "But you know, there are a lot of windows in this house," she said provocatively. "We could test them all out."

He laughed and she joined in.

This had definitely been a good decision, and she wanted more. After dinner.

ELY HEATED UP the dinner he'd brought home—the closest he ever came to cooking. Domestic duties weren't his strong point, but he could manage a microwave. Lydia uncorked some red wine she found in the cupboard. Ely watched her for a second, replaying in his mind what had happened between them less than an hour ago. It still seemed surreal.

She was dressed in thin yoga pants and an oversize sweater that made her look even smaller than she actually was, and he knew she didn't have anything on underneath. That thought made him want to go abandon dinner and strip off those clothes for a repeat performance.

Definitely later.

He wasn't sure what had changed; she didn't seem interested in talking about it—typical Lydia—but when he'd seen her in the window, he hadn't been about to decline the invitation.

Still, it nagged at him. Why the quick switch in her thinking?

They settled on her living room floor in front of a huge hearth where he had started a fire before dealing with the food. Lydia dragged several large pillows and blankets down to the floor, pushing boxes and piles of things she had been sorting through out of the way.

Eating on plates in their laps, they clinked their wine-glasses together and focused on their dinner, enjoying the quiet and the fire. Ely had to say something, finally, since it was clear that she wasn't going to.

"So what changed your mind?" he asked, keeping his tone light as he stole some pad Thai from her plate, popping the succulent noodles into his mouth.

She shrugged. "I had time to think, and I was also tired of thinking. I've been so muddled lately, with the house, my mother, and everything going on. I needed to get out of my head, feel more like myself, I guess."

Ely absorbed that, unsure how he felt about her explanation. So he was her distraction? Though he could understand why she might need that, and why she might need to feel something "normal," he wasn't sure if she had needed him or just someone. If he hadn't been here, would anyone else have done? Kyle? Someone from the bar downtown?

"You said it was fine, that you weren't looking for anything serious, right?" she asked, and he could hear the tinge of apprehension in her voice, as if she were reading his thoughts.

He had said that, and he meant it. Still, describing what had happened between them as "no big deal" bothered him, too.

"I did. I guess I'd like to think it was something of a big deal, at least right now," he said, meeting her eyes, "that you wanted me."

He felt kind of stupid telling her, but so be it.

She smiled a little. "I forget, the male ego is such a fragile thing. Of course it was because I wanted you, and it was very nice."

His eyebrows shot up. "Nice? It was *nice?*"

"I said *very* nice," she corrected, stealing some food from his plate, as well.

"I think it was way better than nice," he countered.

"I'm glad."

He knew she was teasing him, but called her on her bluff, having fun. He liked her when she was playful, which seemed to be far too rare.

"You think you could do better?"

She smiled, and her eyes shone in a way that made her light up inside. He loved it when she smiled like that.

"Are you daring me to make it even better?" she asked mischievously. "Hotter? More satisfying?"

Ely's nerve endings—especially the ones south of the border—were very interested in her dare.

"You couldn't possibly," he said calmly, licking some sauce from his fingers.

"Well, I guess we'll have to see, won't we?" she purred, setting her plate aside and stripping off her top and throwing it to the floor.

Ely set his plate down, too, admiring how the firelight kissed her skin. Her hair fell down, hiding part of her face behind the silk curtain, turning her into an exotic creature focused only on his pleasure.

"What's this symbol here, at the center of the rose?" he asked, letting his fingers trail down her sternum to land on the spot above her navel.

She looked down to where his finger lay against her skin.

"It's a medicine wheel. A Native American friend did that one for me, after we took a drive out into the desert for a week. He said it represented my personal journey, my strengths, and it's also a protective symbol. He told me some other things, too, but it was years ago, and I forget now," she said, touching the mark fondly.

Ely's first instinct was to question. Her friend—was he the kind of friend who also knew her intimately? Intimately enough to put a mark on her that would never be removed? That she still ran her fingers over with a lover's touch?

Down boy, he reminded himself. Lydia was not his—one of the reasons he was so attracted to her was because she was so completely her own person.

"What are you thinking?" she asked.

He looked up at her as she knelt gracefully before him, looking down. Her breasts were shadowed, her back to the fire, only her womanly shape silhouetted by the light coming from the hearth. He was already rock hard and decided not to worry about where her tats had come from. Maybe it was better if he didn't know.

"Just looking at you and taking it all in," he said, reaching up to brush his hand over the taut peak of her breast and loving how she responded so easily, her lips parting to take a breath as her head bent forward. She watched him for a few seconds as he touched her, and then fell forward, pushing him back to the pillows.

"I'm in charge this time, since I have a challenge to answer," she said, her voice smoky.

Then she was kissing him again, her hands unbuttoning his shirt and pushing it away before sliding down over the burgeoning at the front of his jeans. He arched up into her touch, his jaw tense.

"So hard," she said, undoing his jeans.

Lydia took her time touching him, exploring him everywhere. His body was one solid mass of muscle, his cock hot and hard in her hands.

"I would love to create a maze, right here," she said, leaning down to touch her tongue lightly to his solar plexus, making him draw in a sharp breath. "It would wind all the way down," she continued, her tongue tracing the path, "and only I would know where it leads," she finished.

He swallowed hard as her mouth finally landed on the tip of his erection, her light touch reaching down to his root and pulling out a groan of pleasure. She ran her thumb over his shaft, as if exploring him, dragging her nails lightly down the inside of his thighs, to his knees, the back up to stroke him from tip to base. That had him arching from the floor, and as he did so, she took him suddenly and completely into her mouth.

Unable to hold back, he drove himself deeper. She moaned her approval and curled her hands around his backside, holding him there as her mouth worked him.

"Geez, Lydia," he panted. "That's all you got?"

He tried to laugh at his challenge, and was answered as she hummed against him, slipping her hands down in between his thighs to cup his balls, stroking the tender skin underneath with the intention of making him lose control as fast as possible; it was Ely's personal goal in life, the very reason for his existence in that moment, to make this last as long as possible.

"Oh, that's good," he said on a long groan.

Drawing back, she let her tongue toy with the broad crown of his shaft until he was straining against her. He put his hands lightly on her head, not wanting to push, but to guide her just so.

She turned her head to look at him for a second, and the overwhelming heat of her gaze punched the breath from him. Her lips were ripe from kissing him, her eyes molten, hair mussed. She was every man's wildest fantasy, there, poised over him in the most intimate way he could imagine.

"Just let go, Ely. Do whatever you want," she said with a wicked smile as she lowered over him again.

He sighed, given her permission, and wrapped his fingers tightly into her hair as he pressed her down again, her lips meeting the root of his cock. He held her there, and then urged her back up until she knew the rhythm he wanted.

That excited her, too, by the sound of her groan against him. He removed one hand from her hair to caress her cheek, the back of her neck, her nipples, as she brought him closer.

Whimpering against him as she sucked, she shifted her body around, parting her legs so that he knew immediately what she wanted. He wanted it, too.

Lifting her legs up and over him, he put his mouth to her sex, sucking her as hard as she was him. She was salty and hot, slick from his mouth and from her own arousal. It drove him out of his mind. As she went deep on him again, her hands grabbing his backside to keep him there she did…something…that shot him off like a rocket.

He broke contact with her sex, drawing in air as his body buckled, pleasure so intense that he thought he might black out. He might have cursed, cried her name, something—he wasn't sure—he couldn't focus on anything but the orgasm that took over his body, and seemed to last longer than he could remember ever happening in his life.

When it started to fade, he was breathing as if he had

just finished a marathon, his bones turned weak. When he reached to touch her again, his hands were shaking.

Hot damn.

She started to move away, but he stopped her.

"Not done yet," he managed to say and pulled her back to him, sliding down underneath her.

"Ely," she breathed, lifting up to her knees again so that she was poised above him. He parted her with his fingers and found her unerringly. Like she had done for him, he let her set the pace, her hands planted on his stomach as she rocked back and forth. It didn't take long, and then she was crying out his name as she rode it out, finally falling forward over him.

Sliding her hands up his thighs, she levered herself gracefully back down beside him, wrapping her arms around his broad shoulders, and he drew her closer, too.

"That was incredible. Amazing. Heart-stopping. Absolutely better than nice," he said, nuzzling her ear. "Thank you."

She shook with gentle laughter at his side, and nodded. "I think we can do even better…later," she whispered and Ely knew that if he died right now, it would be as a very happy man.

7

LYDIA WOKE UP ON her living room floor as a slant of sun made its way through the window on the wall across from her. She turned over, too comfortable and satisfied to move any farther, her naked body wrapped in the thick blanket and pillows that surrounded her. She and Ely had put some of the big pillows to exquisitely creative use the night before, she remembered with a smile.

She'd slept better last night than she could remember doing in ages. Thanks to Ely, she thought with a smile, stretching long, working the kinks out of her muscles. She smelled like him—like them—causing her body to warm and soften even more, wanting his again. Satisfaction was momentary when it came to Ely—she always wanted more.

Where was he? In the shower? Maybe she could go join him…but listening closely, she heard nothing from upstairs. The house was silent. *Not even a mouse,* she thought with a chuckle.

She didn't even remember falling asleep—but she did remember what had happened before she passed out while snuggled against Ely's warm body. Lydia didn't often actually sleep with her lovers, but it had seemed right this time. They were staying here in the same house, after all. It would have been ridiculous to ask him to go to his own room. There was no need to read any more into it than that.

Startled by the sound of her doorbell ringing, a glance at the clock showed it was after twelve, and she shot up, looking for her clothes on the floor, but only finding her pants. The bell rang again. Pulling them on, Lydia grabbed a blanket, wrapping it around her and pushing a hand through her hair as she called to whoever it was—probably one of the guys—to hold on. She pulled the door open and was shocked to see two women who looked just as surprised as she did.

"Who are you?" Lydia asked, not feeling too congenial as a bitterly cold wind blew up inside the blanket and some snow landed on her bare toes.

"I'm Faith Manning," one of them said, eyeing her curiously.

"And I'm Geri Baxter," the other said matter-of-factly. "You must be Lydia, Faye's daughter?"

Lydia nodded. "I am. Can I help you? Ideally, before I turn into an ice cube?"

"Inviting us in would prevent that," Geri said, not put off by Lydia's directness. She sighed, stepping back and letting them in.

Lydia shivered again. Why was the house so cold? She'd just had the fuel tank filled when she'd arrived.

"So how can I help you two ladies?" They were probably selling something, or whatever. It wouldn't take long to send them on their way.

"We left several messages on your home number and sent a letter in the mail. We didn't have your cell phone," Faith said nervously. The woman looked like she was on her last nerve, pale and tired, with heavy shadows under her otherwise pretty eyes. Lydia wondered if she was ill, and took a step back, her head starting to ache from lack of caffeine and a long night.

She saw both women look past her, taking in the room—the containers of Thai food were littered around, along with the bottle of wine and the blankets all over the floor. The fire in the hearth had long since burned out, and Lydia followed their gazes to Ely's shirt, which was still thrown over the back of the sofa.

It looked like what it was, and Lydia shrugged. She wasn't in the habit of making apologies to strangers for her personal life, and headed toward the kitchen.

"I forget to check the machine. I'm not used to having a landline. Come on in, I need to make some coffee," she said, stopping to put on a pair of her slippers she'd left in the hallway the day before.

The women followed her, and as Lydia attended to the coffee, Faith spoke.

"We were hoping your mother had told you about us, but we weren't sure. We're so sorry to have lost her. This must be a terrible time for you," the younger woman said sympathetically.

"Thank you. Told me what?" Lydia said as the coffee started to brew and she turned to face the two women.

"We're the Winter Festival organizers. Most of the planning is done, but we thought it would be canceled when Faye passed away, and didn't leave any provisions. But I guess she did, since you're here. If you'll allow it, we have to start setting up and solidify the schedule."

Lydia blinked, having no idea what they were talking about.

"Okay. Wait. What does that have to do with me?"

The women looked at each other, clearly tense.

"The town has held the festival here at the ranch for the last few years. It was planned to be held here this year, as well."

Lydia wasn't sure she heard correctly. "That can't be right. The festival was always held in the field at the edge of town."

"Oh, that was stopped years ago. That field was used to build a new child-care center now—didn't you notice?"

Lydia shook her head. She hadn't, actually.

"Your mom always said she was happy to support the town in any way that she could. She enjoyed all the festivity, having people around for that weekend. She really got into it, before she was sick, of course. She would help us plan, bake, decorate, and she became a big part of the festival itself. She even played Mrs. Claus one year."

Lydia was silent, turning to pour some coffee. She asked her two visitors if they would like some, and then poured two more cups.

"See, here are some pictures of your mom at last year's festival. We thought you might like to have them. She said it was hard for you to make it back too often, owning your own business and everything," Geri added, pulling some pictures from her purse. "But we're hoping you're okay with it. It's too late to reschedule anywhere else. If your mom hadn't offered the use of her land, the festival would have been over with years ago. It's hard to find anyone who was willing to host."

Lydia sipped her coffee, but didn't notice the women's curious, subverted glances as they saw some of the ink revealed where the blanket slipped. Lydia stepped up to the table and looked down at the pictures, a hard lump forming in her throat as she saw her mom smiling back from the images on the table. Her mother was with a group of kids building snowmen in one picture, handing out cookies and hot chocolate in another, standing on a tall ladder with several other people helping to hang lights around the barns.

Winter Festival? Here?

There was an older one, and her eyes fell on it. She was standing with her mother, with a huge tray of cookies they had baked for the festival.

"Where did you get this?" she asked, picking it up.

"Your mom used it for one of the posters one year— we thought you might like it back. You were so cute then," Faith said, and then turned red, her eyes widening. "I mean, not that you're not gorgeous now, or anything, just there, you were so—"

"I need to put some clothes on," Lydia said abruptly, putting her coffee down so hard that it sloshed over the edges.

She made her way upstairs and closed the bedroom door behind her, leaning back against it, her breath coming as hard as if she had been running.

How was she supposed to do this? She couldn't do this. She couldn't host a party for the whole town. She wasn't her mother. She had to tell them no. This was too much.

But as she closed her eyes, she saw her mother's face in the pictures. She'd been so happy. Her mom had always loved Clear River, and the Winter Festival had always been one of her favorite events. Of course she would have wanted to host it if it were threatened with ending.

And she'd be disappointed if Lydia was the reason they had to cancel this year.

Lydia grabbed her jeans, heavy socks and pulled a

wool sweater over a thermal shirt, though she was still cold from head to toe as she made her way back to the kitchen.

Faith and Geri looked at her with clear apprehension.

"I'm so sorry, Lydia. I didn't mean that the way it sounded," Faith said, standing and crossing the kitchen to put a hand on her arm.

Lydia looked down at her hand, and Faith pulled it back. Great, now she was scaring the locals.

"Don't worry, I didn't take it that way. I just have so much going on," Lydia said, trying to sound more reasonable. "I have to clean out the house, get it ready to sell. I need to get back to my business in Philly, and this place needs repairs as well as all the daily upkeep. How can I do all of that with the festival, too?" she said, sounding a little more desperate than she meant to.

The women looked at each other and then back a Lydia. "We can help. We have a whole team of people who volunteer to help set up. What if we volunteered to help you get the house cleared out, too?"

"Oh, I don't know," Lydia said, not having expected that and feeling cornered and unsure about having strangers help her with such a personal task.

"Listen, I know this is hard for you, but we can help each other," Geri added practically. "Your mother would have wanted it this way. She told us you might have a hard time coming back here, for a lot of reasons." The older woman paused, giving Lydia a knowing look. "But we were her friends, and so we're yours, too. That's how she would have wanted it."

Lydia nodded, unsure how to feel about the fact that her mother had apparently shared some of her private issues with these women, and had trusted them enough to do so. And here they were offering to help.

She wanted to say no, to decline gracefully, but there was no way she could do all of this by herself. And her mother would have wanted her to help the town. She relented, her shoulders sinking.

"Fine. What do I have to do?"

Geri nodded in approval. "We can go over a schedule with you, and plan in some extra time to help you with the house, to start with."

Faith placed a warm hand on Lydia's cold one. "We loved your mother, and she always spoke so highly of you. I know how hard it can be—I lost my father last year. It can be hard, but it's easier with friends around."

Lydia blew out a breath, unable to argue anymore. She seemed to have friends popping up left and right, whether she wanted them or not.

"Okay, well, let's see what you've got," she said, just as the back door opened, another swoosh of cold air blasting into the kitchen.

Ely appeared in the doorway that led from the mudroom to the kitchen, his gaze landing on the two women at the kitchen table, and then on Lydia.

Heat arced between them, and suddenly her fingers started to warm up, among other things. He looked rugged and incredibly handsome in her father's wool camp coat, brushing snow from his front with hands that had driven her to madness the night before.

"Lydia," he said. "Ladies," to Faith and Geri.

"Morning, Ely," she said, and then realized again that it was actually well past lunchtime. "Faith, Geri, this is Ely Berringer, a friend from back east. He's helping out here, too, for a little while," Lydia said.

Ely stomped the snow off of his boots and kicked them off, walking into the kitchen. Lydia smiled to herself as she watched the women's appreciative glances take in his tall, muscular frame, revealed as he draped his coat over the door. Crisp, dark hair held melting flecks of snow, falling against his forehead and accenting warm hazel eyes and a straight nose. Her heart flipped a little as her eyes landed on his mouth. She wanted to kiss him hello, and struggled to control the urge. He seemed to know as his eyes met hers, the memories of the night before swimming between them. Somehow, she managed to find her voice again.

"Ely, this is Faith Manning and Geri Baxter."

Faith stood, smiling as she linked her arm through Lydia's. She looked tired, still, but happier.

"We're the Winter Festival planners this year. Nice to meet you, Ely," she said.

They shook hands, and Ely's gaze fell on Lydia again.

"We?" Ely said in surprise.

"Apparently my mom offered up the place as the site for the festival. It's too late to reschedule to have it anywhere else," she said, offering a brief explanation.

He smiled. "That sounds fun. Let me know of anything I can do to help," Ely said.

"I'm sure we can think of lots of things for a strong, young guy like you to do," Geri said with a wide grin.

Lydia felt a stirring of something green, her eyes moving to the wedding rings Geri wore. Faith didn't wear any, however.

Ely frowned. "It's freezing in here."

"Yeah, it's been that way all morning," Lydia said, her voice sounding a little more breathless than she liked. Her cheeks warmed as she noted the women watching her, then Ely, with knowing glances.

Now they knew whose shirt was thrown over the sofa in the other room, of course.

"That's actually what I came up to talk to you about. Cold in the bunkhouses, too."

Lydia frowned. "I just had the tanks filled two weeks ago." At significant cost, she added to herself. Fuel oil wasn't cheap. "Something must be wrong with the burners."

Ely's expression turned serious. "I'll kick on the generators and we can start the woodstoves and the fireplace until we can get someone out here to see what happened," he said, grabbing his coat and stepping back into his boots.

"Thanks," Lydia said.

"Wow," Geri said, fanning herself as Ely went back out the door. "If that's how they grow them back in Philly, I think I should have gone to college back east like Mom said," she added.

Faith laughed. "Aw, you know you wouldn't trade Alex for anyone, but I have to second that wow. He's yours?" she asked Lydia frankly. "I can see why you want to sell and go back home. Though he sure fits in here very nicely."

Lydia stammered, unsure how to respond. How to say Ely had only been hers for a night—maybe for as long as they decided this would last—and there wasn't anything else going on?

"We're just friends," she managed, turning to get another cup of coffee.

"I wish I had a friend like that," Faith said with a grin.

Lydia couldn't help but smile. Faith had a way, particularly, of making it impossible not to.

"He's a good guy. But we're not involved," she said, unsure how convincing she was being.

"So you wouldn't mind if I invited him for coffee?

You know, welcomed him to town?" Faith asked innocently.

"No, of course not. He's a free agent."

"Well, then, maybe I'll invite him for more than coffee," Faith said with a wiggle of her eyebrows that made Lydia stiffen initially, but then she noticed the mischief in both women's eyes as they watched her.

"You're teasing me," she said, shaking her head. How could two people she hadn't even known for an hour sucker her in so neatly? Usually only Tessa knew her well enough to do that.

"Hard not to," Geri said, smirking. "You need to loosen up. Get into the Christmas spirit. Hanging about five thousand Christmas lights should do the trick. We'll start that tomorrow. Your mom kept them up in the attic. They need sorting and checking every year, though."

Lydia's jaw dropped. "Five thousand?"

"It's only about fifty strands of one-hundred-count lights…don't worry, not as bad as it sounds," Geri said. "We've done it every year with a few guys who are willing to reach the high spots, up on the roof, and along the edges of the barns."

"Five thousand," Lydia repeated. "And I take it there's room in the budget to pay for the electric bill for running those all weekend?"

"Yes. Money we save by having the site donated," Geri pointed out.

Lydia nodded. "Okay. Then, maybe we can find who's going to be willing to help me clean out the rest of the attic and the basement. I can get the main floors on my own, but I'll need help with those two areas."

Geri wasn't the only one who could drive a hard bargain.

"Done," Geri agreed, and Lydia felt some measure of

relief that she wouldn't be facing all of the house clean-out alone. A delicate chime interrupted their discussion, and Faith pulled a phone from her pocket, frowning, the worry coming back into her eyes.

"I have to take this, just a second," she said, walking back to the front room.

Lydia watched her leave, and then looked at Geri, whose features had also pulled tight.

"What's going on?"

Geri shook her head. "That girl has too much weight on her shoulders. Family problems, her sister, and her nephew—that kid is going to run them all into the ground. Faith even broke up with the sheriff because of it—they had too many disagreements, though he was just doing his job, getting after Roger. But I'm glad you said okay to the festival, because it's the only happy thing she has going on right now."

"Faith was dating the sheriff? Sheriff Granger?" Lydia asked. She remembered Steve Granger from years ago, and noticed he was sheriff right away. Steve was Ginny's brother, and one of the last people she wanted to run into for any reason. It was also why she hadn't bothered filing a report—it was hard to believe that Steve Granger would have any interest in helping her.

"They were pretty serious, and I never saw her happier, but then her sister's husband left, and Julie, her sister, can barely take care of herself, let alone the boy. It all falls on Faith. The sheriff had to arrest Roger one night, and they had a huge fight. He was just doing his job, trying to help that boy, too. She can't see that—she's just trying to protect her family."

Lydia blew out a breath, shaking her head.

"That sucks."

"Sure does."

It made Lydia even more certain that she didn't want to have any of those complications in her life.

Faith came back a few minutes later, looking stressed and saying she had to go. Obviously there was a problem, but Lydia didn't ask what—none of her business, and she wanted to keep it that way. They were nice enough people, and they had an arrangement that would be helpful to her and them, but that's as far as it went. She didn't want to get any more involved than she had to.

8

ELY WALKED INTO the PET heating fuel company, approaching the small desk where an older woman sat with a slick new tablet on the desk, her phone ringing like mad.

Her fingers flew over the shiny screen of the tablet as she fielded the phone calls, making appointments and addressing problems, not even aware of his presence.

Or so he thought. Without looking up, she held up one manicured finger to tell him to wait.

He took in the small office that smelled slightly of petroleum and pine from the small, fresh Christmas tree in the corner. It made him aware of the fact that Lydia had not put up one Christmas decoration, understandable, and very likely to change now that she was part of the Christmas Festival. That had been a shocker.

He couldn't wait to hear the whole story when he got back to the ranch, although talking wasn't perhaps the first thing on his mind. The night before had been insane—one of the best in his life—and he wanted more. He wanted to enjoy everything he could with

Lydia before their time was done, and they headed back to Philly.

Finally, the woman hung up the phone and sat back in her chair, taking a breath.

"Welcome to PET fuel. I'm Millie. How can I help you?"

"Hi, Millie. I'm here to check on an order that was made a few weeks ago, but was never delivered. Woke up pretty cold this morning," he said with a mock shiver.

"Lot of people did," she said with a sigh and a shake of her head. "You'd think they'd prepare earlier. What was the name?"

"Lydia Hamilton? She ordered a fill-up for her mother's ranch a few weeks ago—"

"Oh, I know the Hamilton place, yes. I did take an order for them, I remember—yes, the paperwork is right here—but it was canceled."

"Canceled? By whom?"

"I have no idea—assumed it was Ms. Hamilton herself. I didn't take the call. I saw the canceled order, and just figured maybe she was going with a different supplier."

Ely frowned. "No. She had no intention of canceling, and we really need that delivery," Ely said. "You have no idea who canceled it?"

"Nope. We had a temp on that week, and she didn't take very good notes."

Ely nodded. "Is there any way to get a delivery out there today?"

Millie frowned. "I can put you on the schedule, and it might be tonight, at the earliest. The guys are working around the clock right now with this storm."

"I'd appreciate that," Ely said with a smile, and Millie smirked in return. Not easily charmed, he could see.

"That's a slick piece of hardware you have there," he added, nodding to the tablet.

"Thank you. I finally convinced the boss to get rid of that mammoth desktop computer he had in here and come into the twenty-first century. This little baby does everything I could imagine and more, but I can't seem to get the cash register app to work without crashing."

"Mind if I take a look? We have one that's similar that we use in our business back home, and I think I might know what the problem is."

Millie eyed him up and down and then slowly handed over the tablet. Ely checked out the application and found it did indeed have the same registration conflict as the one they had started using back home. Within seconds, he had fixed the problem, and showed it to Millie in case it happened again.

"That's terrific! Thank you," she said with a smile as the phone started ringing again. "I'll see what I can do to get you moved up in the schedule today, but no promises," she said as she reached for the phone.

"Thanks, Millie," Ely said with a wink, drawing a smile and a shake of the head from the woman as she went back to work.

He was not smiling, however, as he left the office. Someone had clearly canceled the order for fuel with the intention of messing with Lydia again. They were definitely trying to get her out of the house. But why? Smitty told him the water heater had been tampered with, as well. How could someone manage all of this, and leave no path behind? Unless they were at the ranch, he thought, his mind going back to Kyle again.

Picking up his phone, he dialed Jonas's number. After several rings, his brother picked up only as Ely winced, remembering the time change and that it was several hours earlier on the East Coast.

"What?" his brother growled into the phone, and Ely thought he heard Tessa's soft laughter in the background. Ely hoped he hadn't caught his brother and sister-in-law at an inappropriate moment.

"Sorry, Jon. I forgot about the time difference," Ely said.

Jonas said something to Tessa, who murmured something back, and Ely increasingly felt like he was definitely interrupting something.

"Listen, I can call back—"

"No, we're up now. I had to get up anyway," Jonas said, though clearly not happy. "What's up?"

"I was wondering if you had found out anything on that name I gave you? Kyle Jones?"

"Not much," Jonas said, sounding more like himself. "Kind of weird, really. He shows a work history, bank records with paychecks at one of your local banks being deposited over the last seven months, but other than that, he's either been living off the grid, hiding something, or both. I go back longer than seven months and all I find is some sketchy work history and a few creditors, one last known address in California, but not a heck of a lot."

Ely took that in. "Sounds like someone trying to hide their past."

"That, or just a drifter. Picks up work where he can, doesn't have much past to hide. But no criminal record popped up, from his name anyway. If you can send me some prints, maybe I could have my friends at the Bureau take a look," Jonas said.

"Getting tight with the Feds, huh?"

"They have their good points," Jonas said with a laugh. "Lots and lots of resources."

Ely knew that was true.

"Oh, there's one other thing, while I have you on the line."

"What?"

"Guess who's back here for Christmas?"

Ely peered down the main street of Clear River where people walked to and fro, heading to work, running errands, enjoying the first day with no snow since he'd gotten there.

"Have no idea."

"Luke. Just got in a few days ago, came by the office this morning."

Ely let out a whoop, startling several passersby. "That's great. Is he back for a while? I don't want to miss seeing him."

Luke Berringer was their first cousin on their father's side. He'd grown up in New York, and his family had moved to Philly when their uncle had gotten sick. They'd all run together in the same pack as kids. Luke's IQ had always been off the charts, especially when it came to numbers—that led to a special knack for finance, and starting his own investment company by the time he was twenty. He'd been at the top of his game when he'd suffered a personal catastrophe at his office—an employee he'd laid off had killed himself—and Luke had not taken it well.

Closing everything down, he had signed over the business to his VP, letting him buy out his share, and had taken off to find…whatever. The last thing Ely knew, Luke was spending a year in a meditation program in some exotic far-flung place. He could afford it, being wildly, independently wealthy.

"I think he's back for good. He was asking about a job, actually."

"A job? Why on earth would he need a job?"

"He signed over all of his money to various causes and came back to start over. It's something to think about. He has some pretty high-level computer skills, and he picked up some pretty impressive martial arts and language skills on his travels. He might be able to do some white-collar work for us—there's been more of a demand for that."

Ely shook his head in surprise. "I can't believe he gave it all away, and then again, I can totally believe it. He seems to be doing well?"

"As solid as I've ever see him. Different. More focused. More calm. But good. I think he's made peace with it all."

"That's great. It's fine with me, but if you want to wait until we can all talk to him together, I should be back after Christmas."

"Staying on through the holiday?"

"Yeah. Lydia needs some help here, and there's something going on. Someone's giving her a hard time, and I don't know what it's about, but I'll feel better being here until she's back, too."

They continued to talk and catch up when he caught sight of a familiar face—Roger, the young hoodlum he'd seen in the sheriff's office. From the boy's body language—and given the time of day—Ely was willing to bet that the kid was skipping school again and up to no good.

"Jonas, I have to go."

"Sure—you okay?" his brother asked, reading into his tone.

"Yeah, I'll talk to you later. Thanks on Kyle," Ely

said, shutting down his phone and following the kid to see what he was up to as the young man disappeared around the edge of a brick office building.

In the back alley behind the building, Ely saw Roger meeting with another person who was obscured by the hood on his coat. They obviously had some business to conduct. Buying some weed, probably, Ely thought.

But he was wrong, his senses heightening as he saw the older guy hand Roger a paper bag—and a gun. He guessed the sheriff was right: they did have their share of serious problems here in Clear River. A young, disgruntled teen buying a gun in a back alley couldn't be good. Ely continued to watch as the exchange took place, and the older guy left.

Roger tucked the bag and gun inside his jacket and moved to leave the alley. Ely stepped out in front, blocking his path as he did so. The young man nearly barreled into him, and Ely stood solid as the kid caught himself and drew back, making as if to run.

"Aw, kid, don't make me chase you down," he said on a sigh.

Roger eyed Ely warily. "Leave me alone. Who the hell are you anyway?"

"Just someone visiting from out of town," Ely said easily. "But I'm guessing you aren't exactly Christmas shopping back here, and whatever you have in your coat, there, is not a present."

The kid scoffed. "Depends on how you think about it."

"You're a real tough guy, huh? Give me a break," Ely said, staring the boy down. To his credit, Roger didn't blink. The kid had some size, some muscle, though he was no match for Ely, even armed.

"Why don't you show me what you've got?"

"Why? So you can go tattle to your buddy the sheriff?"

"I'm going to do that, anyway, so I might as well get my facts straight. Give it to me."

Roger glared, his cheeks burning red with agitation as he sized up Ely and reached into his coat. Ely tensed, prepared for whatever the kid might pull. He'd learned not to underestimate any opponent when he was in Afghanistan. And Roger definitely had that cornered look.

He relaxed a second later as the kid took the bag out of his pocket, but didn't hand it over. He looked a lot less sure of himself, though.

"Are you a Fed?" he asked, looking a lot more nervous.

"No," Ely said. "The gun, too. Before you hurt yourself."

"My dad taught me how to shoot when I was a kid," he scoffed.

"And he wouldn't want you doing whatever you're doing right now."

"He doesn't care about me," Roger said, looking miserable. "The gun is just for protection. I need to deliver this, or I'm in some deep shit. Like, really deep."

Ely narrowed his gaze, reaching out faster than the kid could react and snatching the bag from his hands.

"What the hell?" Ely said, dumping the contents of the bag on the ground. "You're involved in meth?"

The vials landed in the dirty snow, but a few of them broke. The kid groaned, covering his face with his hands.

"Why did you do that?" he yelled, falling to his knees and scrambling to try to save what he could from the broken vials. The gun fell out on the pavement, as well. "You trying to get me killed or what?"

Ely leaned over and yanked the kid up by the front of his worn coat.

"You were the one who broke into Lydia's house that night, weren't you? And you dropped one of these? Why?"

Studying his face, Ely would be willing to bet that Roger wasn't buying or using; he didn't show any physical signs. That meant he was involved on the other side somehow: supply.

"I want an explanation for this, and then you'll explain again to the sheriff."

The toughness dissolved and desperation took over the young man's expression. "It wasn't me. I didn't break into anyone's place. You don't get it. I'm *dead* if I don't deliver this stuff."

"You're the carrier?"

"So?"

"Why would you do such a stupid thing? Are you out of your mind?" Ely hissed.

"I needed the money. My mom is about to lose the house. Dad took off with his girlfriend, and he's not paying the alimony or the child support. She can't even afford a lawyer to go after him. She's so depressed, all she does is stay in bed all day. I had to do something."

"Ever think about getting a job? Talking to a teacher or Sheriff Granger, and getting some help for your mom, too?" Ely felt bad for the kid, but he needed to know there were sensible options in life.

The boy sneered. "Who's going to hire me? Anyway, they would never pay enough. Not nearly. Then where will we go?"

Ely took a breath and let loose of the kid's coat. He bent down to take the gun. If Roger was telling the truth, he was in a hell of a bind and needed more help than he realized.

"I'll tell you what you're going to do, Roger. You're going to pick that crap up and we're taking it to the sheriff. Then you're going to tell him what you know so that he can close that lab down."

"It's not that easy. You don't understand. These guys are big, and they're all over the county. They can get to me wherever I am."

"That's exactly what they want you to think to keep you in line. Don't fall for it."

"Let me deliver this first, please. I need the cash. Then I can tell him anything he wants to know," Roger bargained, but Ely could see he was just playing an angle.

"No way. This goes no further. You might be broke, but you'll be alive to tell the tale. C'mon, we're going right now."

Roger appeared to cooperate, but they were halfway down the alley when the kid ripped the bag from Ely's hands and took off.

"Damn," Ely spat, taking off after the kid, but losing him almost immediately. Roger had the benefit of knowing the town a lot better than he did.

Taking out his cell, he dialed the sheriff, but as it turned out, Granger wasn't in. He left a message where Granger could find him. Suddenly, his visit to Clear River was getting way more complicated than he ever expected it to be.

LYDIA HEARD Ely arrive, his boot step on the porch already familiar, making her smile. Until she saw he wasn't alone.

Steve Granger was with him.

Ely walked in with the sheriff and Lydia froze, unsure what to say. Had Ely told him what was going on? This was what she had known from the start—Ely cared. He got involved and did the right thing. It was just how he was built.

Steve looked up and saw Lydia.

"Hi, Steve," she said.

"Good to see you, Lydia."

She swallowed hard, finding that hard to believe.

"Thanks. You, too."

"Things been okay out here?" he asked, and she saw something tense in Ely's features.

Dammit.

She straightened her spine. "Things are fine."

He grunted in response, looking at Ely, confirming her suspicions.

"Well, let me know if you need anything."

"I will, sure."

She listened as Ely told the sheriff what happened and handed him the gun. Steve's face grew tight.

"Damn kid. He's going to get himself or someone else killed. I can't believe he landed himself in the middle of this mess."

"He's trying to help his mother, the only way he thinks he can. But yeah, it's bad," Ely said, and Lydia approached, also concerned, especially after what Geri had told her about Faith.

"You don't have any idea where he was delivering the stuff?"

Ely replied, "No. He didn't tell me anything that would help, except that it was a large operation. He said they could find him wherever he was, so he couldn't talk to the cops."

Steve let out a breath. "He's probably right. I'll have

to look for him quietly. If they know we know, they'll get rid of him sooner than later."

Lydia was horrified. "Poor Faith. Does she know?"

Steve looked at her in surprise. "You know Faith?"

His eyes turned a little bleak at the mention of the name. He clearly still had feelings for Faith.

"Only just met her. They're having the festival here," Lydia explained.

"Oh, that's right. Well, she can't seem to understand I'm trying to help the kid, and brushing it under the carpet won't do that. Although, I'm not sure what I can do for him now, except try to keep him alive," Steve said. "I should go. I appreciate your help, Ely."

Ely showed him to the door. Steve turned back to Lydia.

"Ginny told me she saw you at the store."

Lydia froze, aware of Ely's close attention.

"Yes."

"She said it didn't go well, and she was feeling terrible about it."

"I'm sorry for that," Lydia said, waiting for more harsh words of recrimination.

"Charlie can be protective," he said. "But he's a good guy. And she's doing well. Maybe you two should try to talk again."

Lydia tried to smile. "I don't think so. I have a lot going on here, and I'll be leaving soon."

Steve watched her closely for a few minutes, and then nodded. "All right, you know best, I imagine."

When he was gone, Lydia turned her back to the door and closed her eyes.

"You okay?" Ely asked.

"Yeah."

"The other day—at the store—when you were so

upset. Is that what he was talking about?" he asked, putting two and two together.

"I don't really want to get into it."

"Okay," he said, but she could see in his face that it wasn't okay.

"What else did you talk with Granger about?"

Ely's mouth flattened. "I mentioned to him that you had a few problems around the place, and that I wasn't sure it was coincidence. He said he'd keep an eye on things, and that was it. Unless you wanted to do more, that's all he can do."

Lydia's anger was harsh and immediate.

"You had no right. I told you I didn't want him involved."

"Why is that, Lydia? Because he's your friend's brother, and you two had some kind of fight? He seems like a good enough guy, a decent cop—why not let him know you're having some trouble?"

"I'm not talking about this with you," she said, heading for the kitchen. "You have no idea what you're talking about."

Ely followed, as she knew he would, coming up behind her and making her turn to face him.

"He said he was the brother of your best friend, and that things had ended badly. He wouldn't say more, but is that what you're hiding, Lydia? Why you took off? Why someone might be harassing you now?"

Feeling cornered, she shouted, "You need to just mind your own business." Desperate to escape she quickly grabbed her jacket and rushed to the door.

She was out to her car before he could catch her, heading down the driveway. She just needed to get away for a while. Away from Ely's questions and concern, and everything he made her feel.

Out on the road, she switched on some music, and just drove. The roads were more or less dry, and the night was clear. Her heart stopped pounding and her mind settled.

Finally, at the edge of town where all she could see was the endless expanse of snowy fields and starry skies, she stopped and looked out over the emptiness.

What was she doing?

She would have to go back home and face Ely sometime, and that seemed to be the case with everything in her life. There was no more avoiding it. Steve had been fine, and there was no reason to fly off at Ely and run.

Except that there was. She could deal with the way her old friends or people in the town felt about her and what she'd done—she deserved what they thought of her.

But she wasn't sure she could deal with losing Tessa, Ely and the life she'd built for herself now because of it. What would they think if they knew what she had done?

Her cell phone rang and she looked down to see Ely's name glowing in the bright blue screen.

She had to go back. Turning the car around on the isolated road, she drove in the direction of the ranch, and as she got closer, noticed someone had pulled off of a side road behind her. The pickup came up behind her fast, its bright headlights nearly blinding her. She hit the gas, trying to get some distance, but it stayed with her.

Nervous, she looked down again as her phone brightened, Ely calling again. She reached for the phone just as the guy swerved around her, roaring up on her side.

Lydia yelped as the truck pulled closer, crowding her. She held the wheel tight and tried to speed up, but he kept up with her. Then the truck did exactly as she feared, side-swiping her and sending her little Subaru pitching off the road.

She slid into a snowy field, hitting the breaks just as she plowed the front of the car into a massive snowbank, burying the car up to the windshield. Recovering from the impact, which fortunately wasn't hard enough to set off the airbags or hurt her, she looked behind, fearing the person in the truck had stopped and was coming back for her.

No one. Silence and snow was all that surrounded her. The phone's final ring cut through her panicked haze, and she searched for it, locating it under the passenger's seat. She picked it up, trying to control her breathing.

"Lydia, what's going on? Where are you? Why didn't you answer your phone?" Ely asked, sounding at the edge of reason.

"I'm okay, but I'm off the road, and I need help," she said, feeling extraordinarily calm—too calm—until she noted that she couldn't open the doors—snow held them shut.

"What happened? Where are you?"

"About two miles west of the ranch on the main route. Someone ran me off the road, and I can't get the doors open. I'm trapped," she said, panic setting in again.

"Are you hurt?"

"No, I don't think so."

"Just breathe, and sit still. Shut the car off, in case your exhaust is plugged. I'll be right there, with help," Ely said.

"Okay."

Lydia stayed on the line with Ely the whole time he was on his way to her, and he arrived just seconds before Granger did, his lights flashing. Another vehicle came lumbering up from behind, Smitty in the tractor.

That helped enormously as Smitty dug a path to the car, which she could see now was at least twenty feet from the edge of the road, and the guys took shovels to dig around her door, getting her out quickly.

Lydia launched herself into Ely's arms, and stayed close as Steve investigated the scene.

"Can you remember anything about the truck?" the sheriff asked.

"It was big, a double-duty, and black or dark blue maybe," she said. "I never had an angle that I could see the driver or the plate."

Granger frowned. "Trucks like that are probably a dime a dozen out here. I'll check it out, and there is some paint on your car, so we can look for damage on the passenger side of local trucks, but it's a long shot."

Lydia nodded and thanked him as the men attached a chain to her car, and Ely turned it on so that they could back it out of the field. It would be brought back to the police impound, just for a night or two, Granger told her. They'd take pictures of the damage, and see if they could find anything that would lead them to the truck she tangled with.

Getting in the truck with Ely, Lydia was still shivering even though she was warm. They didn't say anything as they returned to the house, but paused in the truck before he shut it off, looking at her with an expression she hadn't seen before and couldn't quite make out.

"You scared the life out of me, Lydia."

"I know. I was scared, too."

"Can you tell me what this is all about?"

"C'mon, let's get inside."

She let him lead her back into the house, but as she

walked up the porch and opened the door, they both froze as they realized the door was already open, left ajar by just the smallest sliver.

Someone was in the house.

9

ELY MADE LYDIA stay by the door as he checked the house to make sure the intruder was gone.

"It's clear," he said to Lydia, noting that the new lock he'd installed had been broken by the forced entry.

Walking out to the lot, he only then noted the larger tire tracks in the snow—two sets, coming and going— so whoever had been here was long gone.

"Can you check around to see if anything is missing? Maybe we can get some clue as to what they're looking for."

"It doesn't look like anything was taken, but then again, the place is kind of a wreck at the moment. It might be hard to tell."

She was right. With her clearing out the house, and the festival preparations going on, there were boxes and piles of decorations and other things just about everywhere.

"The door looks kicked in, so we probably won't find a fingerprint," he said, closing it all the way and blocking it with a heavy cast-iron umbrella stand.

"I just can't figure out what anyone would want. Why

they'd do this," she said, and he noticed her hand shook as she pushed it through her hair.

"Hey, come here," he said, pulling her in close. "We'll figure this out."

He took her coat and hung it, then led her to sit on the sofa.

"I'll be right back," he said, and went to pour them both a large glass of wine.

When he came back, she looked better, some color returning, and he handed her the wine.

"There's more where this came from," he said, hoping for a smile, and getting a shadow of one as he sat down across from her.

"It seems like you might have some idea of what's going on."

Lydia appeared to consider what he was saying and finally, after drinking some of her wine, she started talking.

"Steve's youngest sister, Ginny, was my best friend, but more like my sister. We'd been friends since pre-school."

"The girl in the picture?"

"Yeah. We were…inseparable."

"So what happened?"

"There was a boy I liked. I wanted him to ask me out. There was a spring homecoming dance coming up and all I did was think about him taking me. Ginny knew I was crazy about him, and she promised to see if he liked me, too, in that stupid way we do in high school," she said, with sarcasm in her voice.

"And? Did he?"

"No, she said he said he wanted to ask someone else. I was crushed. So, one afternoon, I had to stay late to take a test I'd missed and when I was leaving, I saw

Ginny—and this guy—kissing by the bus stop. I was so hurt. Even more crushed that she would do that, even more so than him not asking me out. My ego took a hard hit."

"Those are rough years. Something like that, a betrayal, is pretty strong stuff."

"Yeah, well, she tried to tell me that she hadn't done anything. She said he kissed her, not the other way around, but that she liked him, and wanted to go out with him. I was pissed, and should have said fine, but I told her no, if she did that, we weren't friends anymore. After a few weeks of not speaking to her, she begged me to tell her what she could do for us to be friends again," Lydia said, shaking her head in regret, looking down at her tightly clasped fingers.

"Ginny was softer than me, easier-going, tender-hearted. I know now—and I knew then—that I was punishing her for the fact that he didn't want me, but I couldn't seem to control it."

"You were a teenage girl. I don't know firsthand, but I hear they aren't great with self-control," he said with a smile, pushing some hair back from her face.

She didn't look at him, and just shook her head.

"I know it seems silly, but it got worse. I told her that the only way I could forgive her was if she rode her father's prize Thoroughbred. No one was allowed to ride him except for Mr. Granger. The horse was big and high strung. Unpredictable. Very valuable. I had a grand plan."

"You wanted to get her in trouble."

Lydia nodded. "I figured if Ginny was caught even trying to ride that horse, she would be grounded from the dance, and probably for the entire summer. Ginny was always such a good girl, did everything she was told, that I never expected her to agree, really. But she did."

"What happened?"

Lydia swallowed hard. "I should have told her that it was enough that she was willing. I should have stopped her then."

Ely pulled in closer. He had a sick feeling he knew how this story ended, but he wanted to hear it from her.

"What happened, Lydia?"

"She was afraid. We were there with a few of our friends, and we egged her on. Mostly me." Lydia swallowed, her throat tight. "She managed to saddle the horse and get him out to the field, and she was actually doing okay with him. In fact, we were all really impressed. I was…proud of her, and I wasn't even angry anymore. So we clapped, applauding her, and the horse reared. Threw her hard. It just…lost it. The horse was so frantic, she was trampled underneath. I thought she was dead. She was just laying there."

"Oh, babe, come here," he said, trying to provide some comfort, but Lydia was too caught up in the past, and pushed him away. She closed in on herself as if she didn't deserve his comfort. Ely gave her the space, and listened.

"She wasn't dead, but she was paralyzed from the waist down. Permanently. I snuck in to see her at the hospital, to try to tell her how sorry I was, and her father was there. He let me have a good look at what I'd done. He had the horse put down, as well, and he told me his wife was on sedatives. She'd come running to the field when it happened, and saw Ginny after she fell. She had a nervous breakdown. All of it, because of me being stupid and selfish. He told me to go and to never come back."

"Lydia, you can't—"

She held her hand up. "No. There is no forgiveness for some things in life. He was right. I tried to live with it, to make amends, but there was no way to do that. No one at school would talk to me, and while my parents were great, I could see that they were hurt by what I had done, as well. So, I left. I did what Mr. Granger told me to do. I took off, and I never came back."

"Until now."

She nodded. "I did come back to see Mom before she passed on, and she tried to get me to face up to things. Said the hurt passed with time, but she was wrong. It doesn't. I saw Ginny in the store the other day, and it was…bad."

"So that's what had you so upset."

"It's what I deserve. Some things can't be fixed."

Ely frowned at the finality in her voice. Whatever the other woman and her family had suffered, he had a feeling Lydia had suffered just as much, punishing herself over the years just as harshly. She felt she had taken her friend's life—perhaps not literally, but in other ways— away. So she was denying herself any happiness, as well? Was that why she formed so few real relationships? Because she might be happy if she did?

But clearly that had gone on too long.

"I'm so sorry, Lydia, for all of you. But you were a kid, too. You did something foolish, but of course you never meant for that terrible thing to happen. You can't still blame yourself for it. Very likely no one else does, either."

"Oh, they do. Believe me. You should have seen her face, and her husband's face."

"Her husband? So she married?"

Lydia nodded. "I was surprised, too, but Mom said she was doing okay."

"Then why beat yourself up so much?"

"Maybe she made the best of it. Maybe she's even happy now, but that doesn't change what I did."

"Seems to me that you're taking an awful lot on yourself. You made some bad decisions, but we all make mistakes. I saw some terrible things over in Afghanistan, and did some things I may question until the end of my days. I can't tell you about it, but it eats at me if I let it. I try not to let it. It's over now."

"That's hardly the same. You were defending your country, doing your duty. I was just a horrible person. You know the real crappy thing is that I haven't changed much. I took off without a word to Tessa, thinking only of my own feelings. Ginny told me the thing I'm best at is taking care of myself, and she's right."

"You'd just lost your mother. I think Tessa would understand, and Ginny was out of line, the way I see it. She had a bad break, but she also chose to get up on that horse. And that's just how it is."

"I was awful to you, as well," she said. "I'm a disaster as a friend, Ely. People get close to me, and I hurt them even when I don't mean to. If you want to go, I understand," she said.

He shook his head, leaned in, kissing her hair. "I'm not going anywhere. But why would anyone be trying to hurt you now for something that happened over a decade ago? It seems out of proportion, to be reacting this way. Some resentment or angry words, maybe, but not what's been happening."

"I don't know. I can't think of any other reason anyone would want to hurt me," she said, sounding exhausted.

"C'mon. Enough for tonight. I'm going to get some stuff I left in the truck and take a shower. You should join me."

He went outside, and did a little scouting around, just to make sure, before he went back in. Sliding the heavy umbrella stand in front of the door again, he figured it might not keep it shut if someone tried to get inside, but it would make a good crash if someone tried to get in.

Taking her hand and going upstairs, Ely was intent on getting to the bottom of what was happening with Lydia. She'd made a horrible mistake as a teenager, and she had punished herself for it for years—and if someone was trying to drive that lesson home now, he was going to find out who it was, and set the record straight.

THE NEXT DAY, Ely started the day by getting to the home supply warehouse early and replacing not only the lock, but the door, on Lydia's home. Now it featured a solid fiberglass door with a top-notch dead bolt. There wasn't much he could do otherwise, and this made him feel like he was doing something to keep her safe.

He hated feeling helpless, he thought as he put both hands around the thick, wood support he had built into the basement underneath the kitchen floor, replacing the beam it joined above, as well. Satisfied with his progress in the last few days, he removed one of the temporary metal supports that he had in place while he worked. All of the rotted supports were switched out now, and replaced with new. It was a relatively easy, inexpensive fix that would make a lot of difference to new buyers.

Lydia had agreed that something had to be done with the windows; replacement wasn't possible at this point in the season, but he planned to caulk, and he was shocked to find that some of the walls were not insulated. That was a much less expensive fix than new windows, and if she put up insulating curtains, that would help make the place a lot warmer.

He felt good about contributing, and he'd enjoyed the things he'd had to do. In contrast to his bodyguard work, here he got to work with his hands more. When he'd come home from his tour of duty, he picked up with his brothers because it had seemed like the thing to do. They needed him, and he had the skills to do the job they were asking him to do. And he got to be with family. Slam dunk.

But he wondered now, what would he have done if Berringer Bodyguards hadn't been there? What if he had had to come home and figure out what he wanted to do, instead of sliding into a comfortable slot with his brothers?

Maybe carpentry or construction. Or maybe he would have gone back to college for an architecture degree. He'd thought about that once before joining the Marines, but his call to duty had been too strong back then to follow his own personal desires.

Pondering that, he put his tools away and walked upstairs to the kitchen, hearing a soft curse come from the front room. Heading that way, he found her sitting on the floor, buried, almost literally, in Christmas decorations. She didn't look happy about it, either.

The organizing for the Winter Festival that would be held in less than a week had begun in earnest. Hammering echoed from the outdoors where a few guys had shown up to start hanging lights around the barns. Lydia looked at the window and muttered something about the noise.

"They're making such a racket I can't think," she said. "Look at all this stuff. It looks like you just stole

Christmas from Whoville," he said, hoping to make her smile.

No luck. She'd been stressed out to her limit, trying to sort out the house, clearing away the family memories, but also meeting with Faith and Geri about the festival on top of being harassed.

Ely sympathized. If she was feeling grinchy, he couldn't blame her. The holidays were often harder for people who had just suffered a loss, and Lydia was having to literally throw herself into it, when he knew she would rather avoid it altogether.

He made his way through mountains of garland and other decorations, squatting down close to her, and tipping her face up for a kiss. She returned it half-heartedly.

"You know what you need?"

"What's that?"

"To blow off some steam," he said, wiggling his eyebrows. They'd blown off a fair bit of steam in the shower the night before, but he never seemed to get tired of being with her.

Though that brought a small smile to her eyes, she said, "I can't. And I'm not really in the mood. I need to get through all of this before Geri and Faith come over to take inventory on what new things they need to buy, and what was left over from last year."

"C'mon," he cajoled, pulling her to her feet and in for a longer kiss. "It won't take long, but it will be fun. You'll feel better after."

She laughed, which he considered an even bigger victory than a smile, and pulled back to look at him. "Way to sell it, big guy. But what the heck. I could use a little warm-up," she said, desire flickering in her eyes.

She hadn't mentioned their discussion the night before at all. It was as if she wanted to pretend it didn't happen, didn't exist. He went along with that, for now. Though, how to convince her that she shouldn't be punishing herself for what happened so long ago remained a mystery to him.

He wasn't sure that was even his role in her life. They had a good physical relationship—mind-bending sex—and he knew she didn't want more than that, aside from a casual friendship.

That was what he wanted, too. When they went back to Philly, they'd just go on with their lives, and see each other now and then. But for right now, he could try to make things better for her however he could.

"Good girl," he said, kissing her again as he slung an arm around her and headed toward the door.

"Um, Ely, the bedroom is that way," she said, gesturing at the stairs. "Not that a bed is necessary," she added provocatively.

He almost changed his mind, but ultimately stuck with his plan. He knew exactly the kind of adventure that would help get Lydia out of her funk.

Retrieving her coat and gloves from the stand by the door he simply smiled mischievously. "Let's go outside this time."

"Are you crazy? It's freezing out there! We can't, um, do anything out there. And there are people around."

He took her hat, tugging it on over her ears and pulling it down. "Trust me. And don't forget your boots."

Reluctantly, she did as she was told, following him outside.

He pulled her by the hand toward the barn, and she ran alongside to meet his stride. Catching up with him, she looked both worried, and excited, her eyes darting from the barn to the men who waved as they went by.

"Ely, we can't…let's go back inside."

"We can…c'mon," he said, urging her along through the barn and out the back door.

Standing there, she looked at him in yet more confusion.

"Behind the barn? In this weather? No way," she said, starting to turn away to head back in. "Even I have a few limits. Things will…freeze up out here."

"Just wait a second, wait here," he said, and took off down the side of the barn.

Ely hit the edge of the building then doubled back into the field a ways, heading back toward the spot where Lydia stood, muttering something he couldn't hear.

His evil plan in motion, he found a drift that would act as a nice bunker, and picked up some nice fresh snow, packing it into the size of a baseball that he then lobbed through the air—it caught her in the arm, making her jump.

At first, he thought maybe he scared her, and that she thought someone might be bugging her again, but then he saw her eyes narrow, and her hands planted on her hips.

"Ely, where are you?" she called.

He answered with another snowball that hit her in the thigh.

"You're a pretty easy target, just standing there," he taunted from his spot in the snow. The sun was shining down and he actually felt warm even with the frigid reading on the thermometer.

"Oh, don't dare me. You'll wish you hadn't," she threatened, scanning the landscape. Her eyes drifted over him several times.

"I hear lots of talk, but don't see any action," he

yelled, lobbing yet another snowball that smacked into the barn behind her head.

"Oh, you are so dead," she hollered and took off running into the field down behind some large mountains of snow that Smitty had piled up with the tractor.

Ely tried to track her progress—he'd chosen the red hat for her on purpose—but she was so small that she easily disappeared behind the snowbanks. After a few minutes of surveying the field, he started to worry she had perhaps gone back inside and abandoned the fight.

And that was exactly what she wanted, apparently.

A banshee yell from behind him had him spinning around, startled, and her attack plan worked. Standing at the top of a drift behind him, she took advantage of his surprise and pelted him with several huge snowballs, pulling them from her pockets like hand grenades. Only a few missed their aim, the last one smacking him directly in the forehead.

Damn, Lydia would have made a good Marine, he thought, putting his hands up and laughing as he defended against the attack. He had no choice but to mount an aggressive counterattack, and gathered up his own ammunition, heading toward her, running directly into her fire, and launching his own five.

Out of ammo, she was laughing hysterically as he tried to climb the mountain of snow that she stood at, scooping handfuls of snow down toward him as he fought his way up the hill. Ely didn't give up, throwing his snowballs the best he could with the white stuff flying all around him. He was breathless with laughter and the effort of the climb as well once he reached the top.

Lydia clearly knew she was toast and tried to run, but he launched himself forward into the snow and caught her ankle, pulling her down. She landed face-first, as well.

Unmoving, or moving just a little as she pushed one hand down into the snow, she grunted, and Ely's laughter ceased.

"Crap," he said, pushing to his feet—no easy task in the deep snow they were mired in, and making his way to her. He had gotten carried away and played too rough, and kicked himself all the way over to where she was still trying to right herself.

"Hey, you okay?" he asked, and reached to pull her up as best he could, losing his own balance a bit.

She groaned, as if in pain, and he kicked himself even harder.

"I'm so sorry, honey, I—*oof.*"

Ely's words were cut off by a mouthful of snow as she took handfuls and smushed them in his face as if they were a pie, grinning with evil glee.

He'd been had.

Spitting snow, he shook his head as she clapped her hands and laughed even harder.

"Sucker," she said, doing a wiggly little dance, still on her back in the snow in some semblance of a snow angel. A tricky, sexy, sneaky, gorgeous snow angel. "I win," she taunted.

Ely smirked as he looked down at her from where he knelt in the snow and fell down in the snow beside her, picking her up and rolling her over on top of him.

"Yeah, I suppose you did," he said, loving how her cheeks were rosy and her eyes bright. Snow clung everywhere to her, like crystals, and she looked young and carefree—the woman borne of the pretty young girl in the photo on the mantel.

He wasn't sure he'd ever seen her so open, so joyful—not even during sex—and it touched him. It touched him deeply.

"What?" she said, studying his face and sensing his change of mood.

"Nothing. Come here," he said, reaching for her and pulling her down to him.

Holding her tight to him, he found her mouth for a long, warming kiss, touching the tip of his tongue to hers, then exploring deeper as her hands clutched the front of his coat and she sank in.

Ely was aware of the cold snow at his back, and it provided a stark contrast to the heat of her body over him, making him hard in seconds as she moved against him.

"Maybe we should take this inside," she whispered into his ear.

He nodded, unable to take his eyes off of her, sure he had never seen anything as beautiful as her face right there in that moment.

She pushed up, with his help, and he got to his feet effortlessly, as well. He had a lot of motivation to get back to the house, and didn't want anything to shatter the magic between them in this instant. He didn't know what it was, but he hadn't ever felt anything quite like it.

But that was too much to ask for, as it turned out.

As they made their way through the barn—too wrapped up in each other to notice much of anything else—they failed to spot the extra cars parked over by the garage at first.

"Lydia, there you are," a voice called from the porch, and Ely looked up to see two women he recognized— plus a few others—eyeing them with keen interest.

He imagined they made quite the picture, wrapped around each other, soaked from snow, making their way toward the house.

Faith's features furrowed in concern. "Are you okay? You guys are wet to the bone. Did you have an accident?"

To his surprise, Lydia laughed.

"Snowball fight. I won."

The women seemed to not quite know what to do with that information.

"We came over to do inventory, but thought we could also help you start cleaning out a bit, as we agreed," Geri said.

Lydia stiffened in his hold, broke away, smiling stiffly again and saying the things one would say in such a situation. *Of course, thanks for coming, I was just working on decorations, etc.* He watched the women file inside and followed, the magic broken.

He wondered if they would ever be able to get it back.

10

ELY HAD TEASED Lydia that she looked like she'd stolen Christmas that afternoon when he had found her surrounded by all of the decorations she had pulled out of the attic, but now she really was feeling like a certified Grinch.

She'd spent hours sorting through garland, replacing lights on broken strands of blinkers, and listening as Geri and Faith, along with Faith's sister, Julie, and a few others, debated what cookies, treats and activities should be offered.

Lydia was silent as she poked a small blue bulb into the empty socket of the light set she worked on, and watched as Ely worked on windows in the dining room. He had gotten his tools and gone back to his latest task, caulking windows so that when the new insulation was piped in, things would be a lot less drafty. Once he finished that, he'd come over to help them sort through decorations.

Lydia scowled. They could have been upstairs, working off the energy from their snowball war under hot water in the shower or on her bed, but no, here she was playing Santa's elf instead.

True to their word, though, Geri had brought two of her older daughters who were home from college to help with clearing out what was still in the attic. The young women were bright and charming, and they had been working hard at emptying the space out. They'd been polite and dedicated, asking her what should stay or go and packing boxes that now were stacked in the front entryway, ready to be taken to various charities.

Lydia had chosen only one box of items that she wanted to send back to Philly, things she wanted to keep. When she'd come across an old set of woodworking tools of her father's, she asked Ely if he would like them. He clearly enjoyed working with wood, and had seemed very touched by the offer, accepting. Lydia figured he'd earned it, he'd done so much to help her fix up the house.

Her father would have liked him. In fact, Ely reminded her a little of him, in his personality more than his looks. Her father had been a wiry, strong, energetic man whom Lydia strongly resembled with her dark hair, though she was petite like her mother.

Ely had her father's steadiness, though, that solid-as-a-rock quality that made you believe everything would be okay as long as they were around. They were both committed family men who liked to work with their hands. She watched as he laughed with Geri, the two of them stringing popcorn and berries for the Christmas trees. Ely was also slated to go with the men to pick up the trees later that afternoon, and tomorrow they would all spend the afternoon decorating the trees outdoors. On the night of the festival, gifts were put under the trees for local families who didn't have much of their own.

Lydia had donated several things from the house to be given as gifts; Faith assured her that not everything had to be from a store. Many of her mother's things, and the warm coats, especially, were very good quality and in excellent condition, and would be appreciated as gifts.

Unlike her, Ely really seemed to be enjoying himself. He bent down to pick up something from his toolbox, neatly snipping the string and tying it off. As he did so, his eyes met hers across the room, and he winked. It was so fast Lydia thought she might have missed it, but then he bent down to the floor, apparently for her benefit, his jeans showing off his perfect butt. That made her smile; he was such a goof.

Geri caught her attention, and smiled, too, as if the older woman knew exactly what was going on. Lydia went back to replacing her lightbulbs. She and Ely may have missed their chance earlier, but maybe things could rekindle later, after everyone was gone, she thought hopefully.

Feeling suddenly antsy, she stood, letting the string of lights fall from her hands.

"Are you okay, Lydia?" Julie asked, noticing her abrupt movement.

Faith's sister had clearly been through the ringer, and from what Faith said, it was a miracle to even get her to leave the house. Julie's husband had left her, Roger was in trouble, and she was about to lose her home, and Lydia's self-indulgent agitation disappeared. Lydia had no problems at all compared to what Julie was going through.

Faith seemed happy that her sister was here, but tense,

as well, bending over backward to get her involved, cheer her up. Lydia supposed she could stop being such a crank and help with that.

"I'm fine. I just need to stretch my legs. I'll be right back," she said, needing a few minutes to herself, but also thinking she could make some hot chocolate while she was in the kitchen. Her mother's recipe was the best in the world, and everyone deserved a treat. As much as she wasn't in the Christmas spirit, Lydia would never have been able to get the attic cleared out on her own, and the girls had done a great job, finishing it in a day.

This was one way she could say thank you, she thought, putting on a huge pot of milk and mixing up the chocolate powder, sugar and spices. Brown sugar and cinnamon were secrets to her mother's recipe, along with lots of vanilla, and Lydia improvised a bit, adding her own spice.

Soon, the kitchen smelled heavenly. Lydia was setting out mugs on the counter when the swing door that led into the kitchen creaked, and she turned to find Ely crossing to her. Without preamble he pressed her into the counter with all six-foot-plus of his body and captured her mouth in a surprise kiss that made her toes curl.

She forgot about everything else in one second flat and snuggled in as close as she could, wanting to swallow him whole.

"Something smells amazing in here," he said against her neck, jerking her back into the moment and reminding her that if she didn't want to start from scratch, she had to turn the heat off under the pot.

She pushed away, reluctantly, doing just that.

"You almost made me burn the chocolate," she scolded, taking the pot off the heat and going to search the refrigerator for some of the canned whipped cream she had seen in there earlier.

"Ah, there it is," she said, reaching in and grabbing it, turning back to find Ely pouring the hot chocolate into mugs.

He was like that. He just jumped in and helped, like it was the most natural thing in the world.

"Thanks," she said, poised with the whipped cream and cinnamon sugar to put on top.

"This is incredible," he said, rubbing his finger along the side of the pot and licking it, his eyes closing with a low moan.

Lydia's blood pressure skyrocketed, watching him. He swiped some more of the chocolate and offered it to her. She accepted it, drawing his finger in, watching his eyes darken as she let her tongue play a little before she let him go.

"That *is* good," she said huskily.

He looked like he wanted to jump her right there and then, and it made her smile. "Help me carry these in?"

"Only if you promise to save some of that whipped cream for later."

"I promise." No problem there. She grinned.

They carried in trays of the steaming hot chocolate, greeted with gasps of surprise and pleasure, and Lydia felt herself blushing under the profuse praise everyone offered as they enjoyed the treat.

"It's Mom's recipe. I just put it on the stove," she demurred, but they continued to sing her praises.

"Your mother often made hot chocolate for one of the festival booths, and cookies, too," Geri commented. "And it was always delicious, but you added a little something else here, didn't you?"

Lydia nodded. "I went to Mexico once on vacation,

and they like to put chili pepper in their chocolate. I put a tiny amount of cayenne in there, just to spice it up, but not too much, I hope?"

Geri rolled her eyes back after taking another sip. "Not too much at all. This is transcendent. Thank you."

Others echoed her sentiments, and Lydia hoped they weren't going to ask her to make the chocolate for the festival. She didn't mind helping prepare, especially in trade for help with the house, but she had no plans to attend, herself. She couldn't bear the idea of people's curiosity and questions, or possibly bumping into Ginny or any of her family. She figured she would spend the weekend in town, or at least, in the house, working.

Getting ready to go.

"Lydia, did you hear?" Ely prompted, leaning in and nudging her with his knee.

"What? I'm sorry, I was lost in thought."

"Well, we were hoping you would make your hot chocolate for the festival, but then Megan had a better idea," Faith said, smiling at Geri's eldest daughter.

Lydia's hopes failed as she realized she wasn't going to be able to sidestep the issue after all. She imagined they weren't going to be very happy after she had to refuse to take part, and in front of everyone here who had been so happy a few minutes before.

Megan smiled excitedly. "Laura and I had the idea, actually," she said, crediting her sister. "We thought you could do tattoos for the festival. Not real ones, but temporary, like they do at the fair. Henna or something. We love yours," she said admiringly, her eyes landing on the ink that was visible on Lydia's arms and throat, revealed by the T-shirt she had changed into after coming inside.

"Oh, I don't know that anyone would—"

"Oh, they would! My friends would all want one, and I want one. We could charge something that would cover your supplies, and the rest could go to the local horse rescue organization, or whatever charity you want, but Laura and I were hoping you could help support the horses," Megan said. "Things are tough for them this time of year."

"Megan is studying to be a large animal veterinarian," Geri said proudly. "Laura wants to be a teacher."

All eyes on her, Lydia froze, unsure how to respond.

"I don't know. I would need supplies, and I probably couldn't do it outdoors, the ink would freeze, and it could be expensive—" she stuttered, flustered and trying to find a way to get out of this.

"There's a place in the city that has supplies," Laura said easily, so intent on their plan that they didn't even notice Lydia's anxiety. "We can make sure to charge a price to cover them, and you could have a booth in the garage, with a heater, so it would be comfortable," she said, defeating every one of Lydia's arguments.

"Um, well," Lydia said, still scrambling for something to say other than that she didn't want to.

"The horse rescue really needs the funds. I kind of promised them that we'd find a way for the festival to help," Megan said, clearly more apprehensive, noting Lydia's lack of enthusiasm.

"We can get one of the other vendors to put in a percentage," Geri said, clearly stopping her daughters from applying too much pressure.

"But, mom, the tattoos would bring in so much more, and it would help so many more of the horses," Laura said, clearly not wanting to give up.

Lydia was trapped. How could she say no to rescue horses? She'd had a horse of her own that her father had rescued when she was a girl, and she knew what the animals suffered if organizations didn't help them. She made regular donations through her business to many charities, but here she had a chance to act directly, through her art.

"I could probably only do very small, pre-patterned tats, nothing too fancy," she said haltingly. "But the supplies are on me. I don't want to take any of the donations away from helping those horses."

Ely squeezed her thigh in approval, and much to her surprise, Megan and Laura launched themselves at her, knocking her back on the sofa in a full-body hug with profuse thanks.

The girls were even more psyched as they went back to work and cleared up the mugs as the preparations for the festival continued. Ely was heading out with the guys to go pick up the load of Christmas trees, and before he went, he dipped down to kiss her—in front of everyone.

"See you later," he said close to her ear, and added, "You're doing a good thing. You have a good soul, Lydia," he said, kissing her on the temple, leaving her feeling flustered.

Then he was out the door, and Geri, Faith, Julie and the rest were staring at her with knowing glances.

"You are one lucky woman, Lydia," Faith said with a gusty sigh, watching Ely leave.

"I told you, it's not like that, we're only—" She stopped and noted Geri's cautioning gaze toward her daughters, whose ears were perked in their direction. "Friends. We're only friends."

"Yep, that looked very friendly to me," Julie said, really smiling for the first time that night, and they all laughed.

Even Lydia felt a little flicker of Christmas spirit, in spite of herself. Or maybe she was just looking forward to using that whipped cream with Ely when he returned home later.

"LOOKS LIKE WE HAVE one extra," Ely said, surprising Lydia as he came through the door dragging a humongous tree behind him.

Lydia had managed to clean up most of the detritus from the decorating and the work on the house, and she watched as he stood the tall tree up in a corner by the front windows. For a moment, she was blasted back to the past, remembering when she and her father used to do the same thing, going out to find the perfect tree, taking it home and standing it up in that very spot.

"But…I don't need a tree," she said.

"Everyone needs a tree. They had extra at the farm, and I couldn't resist. God knows we have enough decorations," he said. "C'mon, it will be fun."

Lydia knew she was going to cave. The tree was perfect.

"I'll go fish out the stand I found earlier," she said, heading down to the basement.

A few minutes later, they had the tree standing on its own in the corner, admiring its shape before they decorated it.

"I haven't had a tree in so many years, I forgot how much I like them," she said as she reached forward to touch the bristly needles.

"Well, you have about a dozen outside, and I'm glad you like this one. I picked it out myself," Ely said, his hand resting at the nape of her neck under her hair, where he massaged her gently.

"This one has to be the prettiest," she complimented, enjoying the moment.

"Not as pretty as you," he said, leaning in for a kiss.

She laughed at the silly compliment. "Sure, compare me to a tree."

"And one with needles at that," he said with a grin, earning himself a playful punch to the middle.

They both began to pull out a few of her family's decorations—not the ones for festival use—and before long, the tree looked magnificent, lighting the room with twinkling lights all reflecting off of many ornaments she remembered from when she was a girl. Ely had built a beautiful fire in the fireplace, and everything was just perfect.

And not.

Lydia felt her throat constrict, and didn't realize her hand had tightened considerably on Ely's as they admired their work.

"You okay?"

"Yeah, sorry," she said, feeling like an idiot and swiping at her eyes. "My mom would have loved this. She loved Christmas, and decorating the tree. Many of these ornaments were her favorites."

"Then that makes it even more special," Ely said, slipping his arm around her and bringing her in close.

That didn't help, and Lydia was helpless to stop the rush of emotions that surged to the surface.

"I should have been here more. I wasted so many years. I should have been home for Christmas," she said, tears coming whether she wanted them to or not. She buried her face in Ely's shoulder, and let them, and he simply held her while she did.

When she calmed down a little, they stayed that way, and she sighed against Ely.

"I'm such a mess," she mumbled against his sweater.

"You're allowed," he said, and didn't try to fix things or tell her what the answers were.

He was just there.

"What would your mom say to you now, if she was listening in?" he asked.

Lydia thought about it. "She'd say don't cry over spilled milk, and that carrying around regrets doesn't help anyone," Lydia answered honestly. Her mother had told her that more than once over the years. "She'd probably also say why are you crying and being all morose when you have that hot hunk of a man in your living room and a can of whipped cream in the refrigerator?"

Ely pulled back and gave her a look that made her laugh.

"Well, okay, maybe not the whipped cream part. That was mine," Lydia said, feeling lighter again.

"Your mother sounds like she had her priorities straight," Ely said, and nuzzled into her neck, making her sadness burn off in a whole new wave of sensation.

"I've done a lot of things, but none of them by the light of a freshly decorated Christmas tree before," she whispered provocatively in his ear.

"I'll get the whipped cream," Ely said without preamble and was gone so fast he left her laughing again.

Closing the curtains and stripping down to her undies, Lydia had a sudden burst of inspiration and dug quickly through one of the festival boxes, retrieving a fur-lined Santa hat and strap-on white beard that she'd remembered seeing there. She put them on and then launched herself onto the couch, affecting a sexy pose just as Ely turned the corner into the room.

"So what do you want for Christmas?" she said in a low, Santa-like voice.

He made a full stop, his face crumpling into more laughter as he stripped down and joined her. Lydia knew it was a long time since she had laughed as hard as she did as she tried to kiss him through the faux beard. Finally, it was removed and Lydia was glad as Ely took full possession of her mouth with no obstacles between them.

Their underwear went the way of the beard and their other clothing as Ely made his way down her body, her giggles dissolving to sighs. As he grabbed the can of whipped cream, he sent her a hot look and a wicked smile.

"The hat can stay on," was all he said before his mouth and his hands made her lose her mind, and Lydia was happy to let him.

11

ELY THOUGHT HE might be hearing jingle bells, but then realized it was his phone ringing. Somewhere.

Lifting carefully up from the sofa where Lydia was curled up sound asleep, he looked at the clock and saw it was a little past ten. Throwing a few more pieces of wood on the fire, he stoked it to keep the room warm. The oil company had delivered their fuel, but Ely loved the heat from the fire.

"Yeah?" he said, grabbing the phone from where it had fallen out of his jeans pocket on the floor, not bothering to see who it was.

"Ely," Jonas said, sounding serious.

"Jon. You're up late. Everything okay?" he said, stretching. Lydia had exhausted him.

"Just catching up on the day and I figured you'd still be up. I just got a report faxed to me from a buddy at the FBI—I called in a little quid pro quo for the project we're working on now, and he did some digging—some deep digging, on your guy, Kyle."

Ely's tiredness evaporated as he grabbed his clothes and pulled them on.

"Tell me."

"He's undercover DEA," Jonas said gravely. "His real name is Ian Riley. There's a drug cartel running a daisy-chain of meth labs all over the Midwest, and Clear River has been targeted as one of the locations. What did you land yourself in the middle of, there, Ely?" he said, clearly worried.

Kyle? With the Feds, and a Drug Enforcement Officer at that?

And on Lydia's ranch? Was this just his cover, or was Lydia in more danger than they had thought? But why?

"I can't imagine how Lydia or the ranch is caught up in any of that," Ely said, telling Jonas about what had been going on. "Maybe they suspect Kyle—Ian—and that's drawing heat in her direction?"

"No, if they did, they'd just kill him."

Ely's blood ran cold as he looked back to where Lydia lay sleeping.

"It gets worse."

Ely's attention sharpened. How could this get worse?

"They aren't sure if he's completely clean anymore. You know how it goes. He hasn't been reporting back, and they don't know if he's still working on the right side."

Ely closed his eyes, thinking of all the times he had left Lydia alone here on the ranch with Ian.

"I'll find out."

"Better if you two just pack up and get back here. Let the Feds work it out."

Ely shook his head. "She can't. She'll lose her inheritance—her mother stipulated she had to stay here for a month."

"Why?"

Ely pinched the bridge of his nose, not wanting to

break Lydia's confidence, but he'd already done that to some extent. "Her mom just felt she needed to come home and deal with some things from her past, and Mrs. Hamilton was probably right. But I don't think she realized there was a drug cartel involved."

"Damn. Okay, well, lay low, then, until you can leave. Only a few more weeks?"

"Should be able to leave a few days after Christmas, and I know Lydia is eager to get back."

That reality dug at him a little.

"Okay, good. How about you? You okay?"

"Yeah. I'm fine. There's a lot going on," Ely said, filling Jon in about the festival.

"Well, that's good—that there will be a lot of people around. Just stick close, and I'll let you know if I hear anything more."

Ely frowned. "No problem there."

They hung up, and Ely stood, his entire frame tight, on alert, and he knew exactly what he was going to do. Jonas might not think it was a good idea for him to confront Kyle—or Ian, whoever he was—but Ely was going to find out exactly what was going on. He grabbed his jacket and headed out the back door.

Snow was falling again, and he stepped silently, checking the door of the bunkhouse. It was open. Stepping inside, Ely took in the lodgelike surroundings. Not so much a bunkhouse as a large log cabin. He took a few minutes to search the place, noting the half-gone bottle of Jim Beam and a couple of glasses on the coffee table in front of the television. Not a bad option to keep warm.

Poking around, he found nothing unusual. A stack of papers on the small kitchen table told him Smitty was paying his bills on time. Other than that, he found out what magazines the guys liked reading and what they drank and watched on TV. There was next to nothing about Kyle—Ian, he reminded himself—left around. The guy was careful.

Ely was silent as he made his way to the second floor. Recognizing a flannel shirt that Smitty favored hanging on one of the doorknobs, Ely checked the other rooms until he heard loud snoring. Opening the door carefully, Kyle was stretched out, dead to the world.

Ely approached the bed, shutting off his mind and his senses to everything but the man in front of him. He struck quickly, pinning Kyle down by the throat at the exact same second the man lunged upward. Ely had already retrieved his handgun from under the pillow, and pointed it at him, lifting a finger to his lips.

Kyle nodded slightly, wary and still, pulling back toward the pillow.

Ely moved to the door, shut it and kept the gun on the other man, taking a seat in a chair by the desk.

"So, *Ian,* let's talk," Ely said easily. Dangerously.

"I should have known you'd figure it out," Ian said. "You seem like the type."

Ely didn't let him deflect the conversation back in his direction.

"There are some folks back in D.C. who think you might be a little too far in. That the case?"

To his credit, Ely thought the surprise on Ian's face was real.

"No way. I had to stay low. I think someone's watching, and they should know I can't risk reporting in," he spat, his eyes angry.

"So what is going on, and how is Lydia catching flack on this? Is it because you're here?"

"I think they want something here. On the property,

in one of the buildings, I don't know. I've searched the fields, the barns, and I can't find anything."

"That leaves the house. Someone was in there last night. You?"

Ian nodded.

"You find anything?"

"Not a damned thing, but you came back too fast. I didn't look through it all. Maybe there's nothing there."

"I found a vial outside the house the day after the first break-in," Ely said. "That yours?"

"Crap, I wondered where that was. It must have fallen out of my pocket when I was hauling you around. I was sending it back for evidence. Found a cache of them at an abandoned ranch about five miles down."

Ely just didn't know whether he could believe the guy or not. Ian was a trained undercover operative; he was a professional deceiver. But Ely had no choice but to work with him for the moment. *Keep your enemies closer.*

"Maybe it's not related," Ely said. "Lydia had some trouble back when she was a kid—"

"Yeah, I know. Faye told us about it. Tough break."

"Could be someone doesn't want her around. Maybe this has nothing to do with the meth."

Ian's expression changed, revealing that he hadn't even considered that. "I guess it's possible though it seems unlikely. After all this time?"

"Yeah, I know. But people can hold grudges for a long time."

Ian nodded. "If you can get her out of the house again, for a longer time, maybe overnight, I can do a proper search and we can know for sure. If there's nothing in there, then I can't think of any other reason they'd be sniffing around here."

Ely agreed. "Okay. We'll do it your way. We have to go into the city to get some supplies tomorrow. I'll make arrangements to be gone overnight."

Ian's eyes glinted. "Yeah, I figured there was something like that going on. Had my eye on—"

Ely leveled a gaze, cutting him off. "Watch yourself. I still have the gun."

Ian laughed and put his hands up.

"You may not be able to report back to your people, but I can report to mine—and I'm going to," Ely warned. "So don't think you can pull anything, Ian. You aren't operating solo anymore, and if anything you do so much as harms a hair on her head, I'll make sure you regret it."

Ely took the clip out of the gun, shoved it in his pocket and shot the empty weapon back at the guy before he could respond and left. Sprinting back to the house, a plan formed to get Lydia away from the ranch for a night. He didn't like lying to her, but it was probably best if he kept what he knew about "Kyle" to himself until they had a better idea of what was going on. She had enough on her mind, and the less she knew, the safer she would be.

Ely would make sure of that.

ELY DROVE THE Subaru into Billings, putting his worries behind him for the time being. Lydia had seemed to tune in to his tension that day as they had worked with other people from town, decorating trees and putting the final touches on the ranch for the festival. He'd been surprised by her perceptiveness, or that he was losing his touch, and letting himself be so easily read.

For now, they were just going to enjoy the chance to get away from the town for a while. He'd talked with

Jonas, who wasn't thrilled, but it had been Ely's call. He was the one here in the middle of it.

The timing had been perfect. Lydia needed to get supplies for her tattoo booth, and he had been put in charge of running some other errands assigned by Geri. Ely had planned a night away that would be good for both of them, and he was looking forward to having Lydia to himself. The festival was only three days away, and Christmas the next week. Then they would go home, and all of this would be over.

"I should check with the insulation company and make sure they're still coming out as planned," he said, making casual conversation.

"Okay, that shouldn't be a problem. We'll want to get back as soon as we can, though. I heard there was more snow coming in."

"Never-ending supply of the stuff here," he said with a smile.

"Yeah. I'm kind of getting used to it."

He made his way down through the main drag of the city. Lydia had offered to drive, but he knew she was tired, and she had napped for part of the trip. Good. Because he hoped they would be up late that night. He planned to make the most of every minute they had left.

"So, what first?"

"Let's find the tattoo shop that Megan mentioned and we can get the supplies, and we'll go from there," she directed.

So before long, they were at their first destination. The shop was well lit with true light, Lydia mentioned, so that colors were not distorted; that helped consumers know what the tattoo would really look like when it was done. The walls were covered with designs that people could choose from, and also pictures of people who had gotten their ink in the shop. A second room to the back offered various kinds of tattoo shop necessities, including the ink and supplies that Lydia would need for the festival.

Ely was fascinated to listen in while Lydia conversed with the owner, an older woman named Dot, who had as many tattoos, if not more, than Lydia. A transplant from New York who had followed her husband to Billings for his work, Dot and Lydia seemed to bond immediately. She and Lydia spent a few minutes admiring each other's art and technique, discussing their shops and so forth. Lydia was in her element, it was easy to see; it was the first time she had relaxed in days, Ely noticed.

"Listen, since this is for a good cause, I'll give you the twenty percent discount I give to other shop owners," Dot said at the register. "After all, it is Christmas. And we won't be here after the New Year, so it will be good for me to clear out some inventory."

"Thanks," Lydia said warmly. "But why are you closing down?"

"Frank can't take the cold and the snow anymore. We're moving south, and I may just work on a freelance basis. Time to enjoy some of the finer things in life," Dot said with a smile. "I'll miss this place, though. And business has really picked up in the last few years. Everyone and their sister wants tattoos now. I did a whole bridal party last week," she said, laughing.

After they shared a bit more information, the women parted ways and Ely and Lydia headed out. Lydia stopped by the bin of toys by the door.

"Toys for Tots," Ely said, walking up behind her. "We donate a lot every year from Berringer. It's always fun doing the toy shopping, since we have no kids in the family right now, though I get the feeling Tessa and

Jonas will be changing that. But it's fun to do the shopping and the donations."

"You think they will have kids right off? Tessa didn't mention it, and she's so busy with her shop," Lydia said with a frown. Tessa would be a great mom—and Lydia an honorary aunt—but she couldn't imagine how someone could balance both, and she also couldn't imagine giving up her life's work.

"Oh, I imagine they would figure it out," Ely said easily.

Lydia had never really considered having her own kids; probably because she never really considered being in any long-term relationship other than her few friendships. Being an aunt could be fun, though, if Ely was right about Jonas and Tessa.

Heading out the door, Ely took Lydia's bag, in spite of her protests that she could carry it on her own, and they walked back toward the car.

"Why don't we go toy shopping?" Lydia said suddenly, stopping on the sidewalk as "All I Want For Christmas Is You" piped along the streets from some unseen speaker. "We can donate some to the toy drive here, and bring a bunch back to Clear River for the festival, for the kids. I know Faith said the stuff we donated from the house was good, but kids should have new toys," she said.

Ely was surprised at her suggestion, but he liked it. Turning to face her on the walk, he said as much.

"You were inspired by the toy bin?" he asked.

"I guess. I normally do all of my shopping online and avoid stores at the holidays like the plague. But you're here because of me, and probably missing that shopping trip with your brothers. And I would like to contribute new toys to the festival."

"I think that's a great idea, though you don't have to worry about me being here. I'm happy to be here," he assured her. In fact, he couldn't think of anywhere else he would rather be. The place, and the woman, were growing on him very quickly. A little warning bell went off in his brain, but he ignored it, opening her car door for her.

"Let's get these next two boring stops out of the way, and then we can hit the west end of the city where the main shopping is for toys."

"How do you know that?"

"I picked up a bunch of local maps and tourist stuff when I was here at the airport. Always nice to know your surroundings," he said, putting the bag in the back-seat and opening the door for her.

They made their way through the city, bickering humorously as Ely refused to use the GPS Lydia had in her purse—at first—until they ended up in a puzzle of one-way streets that kept them going in circles for a while. Once he gave in, they made their way across town in some of the craziest traffic he'd ever been in, arriving safely at a boulevard with as many stores and plazas as he could imagine.

"This place always has good prices," he said, pulling into the lot of one of the major discount stores.

It took a while to find a space—the place was crowded—but they finally did. Ely realized that Lydia was right; he had missed the toy-shopping trip with his brothers, and he was looking forward to this, especially with her.

Slinging his arm around her shoulders, they hurried across the lot as the wind picked up, slicingly cold as they reached the doors.

"Oh. My. God." Lydia breathed, taking in the crowds and the lines.

"Well, it is almost a week before Christmas. Still up for it?" he asked, watching her closely.

She nodded, resolute, and said, "It's a good thing I brought a bodyguard, though. If they stampede, I guess you have to throw yourself in front of them to save me, right?"

He laughed. "Yeah. I think we'll just make use of some strategic avoidance techniques instead," he added, taking her hand and leading her through the store, weaving a path of least resistance through the crowds.

"Over there." Lydia pointed and to his surprise, Lydia gravitated directly to the dolls and he heard her whisper "yes" as she spotted something placed up high on the shelf.

"What did you find? You look like a woman with a mission."

"Ink Baby," she said with glee. "How can I resist?"

"Is that the one that caused such an uproar a few years ago?" Ely asked, and smiled at the surprised look she sent him.

"I was in the Middle East, but we had the internet," he added.

"Ah, I guess I didn't figure you followed consumer news," she said. "But no, this is different. That one was a Japanese limited edition. It had the tats on the doll, complete with a spike collar, off-the-shoulder shirt and a spiky little dog on a chain," she said. "It was cute. I actually have one, new in box."

Ely was amazed. Another interesting secret about Lydia—she liked dolls. He never would have guessed that in a million years.

"And how is this one different?"

"This one includes tats as stickers that the kids can apply or not. The clothes are also more girlie, so you could just forget the tattoos altogether, but why would you? That's the fun of it."

"And no spikes or collars," he added.

"Right. Though I don't know what all the fuss was about. When we were kids, the bubble gum would sometimes come with the temporary tattoos you could put on if you licked your skin and pressed them on. We loved them, and no one cared. What's the harm?"

Ely looked her up and down in a blatant, lascivious way, and she laughed, putting several boxes in the cart.

"Let's also buy some Hex Bugs or construction sets that we give to boys and girls," she added.

"And Matchbox car sets. Have to have those," he added.

They also bought several yo-yos and containers of Play-Doh and Silly Putty.

"I like classic, simple toys. They teach kids not everything has to be expensive or fancy, and can still be loads of fun. My parents bought us Slinkys for every Christmas, mostly because we would try to walk them or hang them off of everything during the year, and always needed a new one by the next," he said with a laugh.

"It sounds like you had a great childhood."

"I can't complain. We had our up and down times. My Dad lost his job once, and that was hard. Jonas had trouble with the department, of course, and then Garrett lost his wife—some tough times, but I think we got through them because of all the good stuff that came before that."

"Garrett met someone in San Francisco, Tessa said," Lydia commented.

"Yeah. Tiffany, I think her name is. I don't know much since I was out of touch, but I guess she's a private detective, and he's completely besotted, from what I can tell, and it's about time. We all wondered if he would ever find someone after Lainey."

"That's so nice that he's in love again," she agreed. "Is he staying there?"

"Only for Christmas, so she can be with her family before they move back here."

"Your brothers are falling in love like dominoes," she said with a laugh.

"Jonas and Garrett were ready, I think. I can't imagine Chance ever settling down. He's got plenty of women, but just like everything else, he's in it for the adventure. Once that wears off, he moves on."

"I wondered. He's not home much, is he?"

"Not if he can help it. He likes to take the jobs that require more travel, which is good, given that both Jonas and Garrett will be staying closer to home now."

"What about you?"

"I don't mind the travel, but I've been thinking I might not want to stay in the bodyguard business permanently, either. I have some other goals I might look into after the holiday. Maybe talk with the guys about working part-time."

Lydia's surprise showed in her face. "How do you think they'll be with that, especially since you're starting to get some pretty big jobs?"

He shrugged, ignoring the prick of guilt at the back of his mind as Lydia voiced his own concerns. He didn't know how his brothers would react, either, and he hated the idea that he might be letting them down.

"Well, we might be able to hire on, I guess we'll have

to see," he said vaguely, steering their overloaded cart to the checkout area.

They left the subject at that, and Ely was glad. He was having a great time. As they chatted about their purchases and the festival, he realized that even standing in a long line at the store was fun when it was with Lydia. The thought should have worried him, but he pushed it away. Jonas and Garrett were ready to settle down, but Ely wasn't—that hadn't changed. Right now, watching her smile and unload toys with him onto the counter, he just wanted to enjoy the moment and was looking forward to the night ahead.

LYDIA HAD HAD a blast while toy shopping, even amid the craziness of the crowded store, more than she ever imagined she could. The back of the Subaru was packed with their purchases and then they had stopped to buy more wrapping paper, bows and tape. This added more work to her already heavy to-do list, but she was so excited to imagine the kids finding their new toys under all of the trees. They would be wrapping gifts for hours tomorrow.

She was almost looking forward to it, smiling at the sneaky bit of Christmas spirit that had worked its way into her life. Maybe it was because she was doing all of this with Ely, as well as Geri, Faith and the others. In previous years, she had faced the holidays alone, in spite of Tessa's frequent invitations for her to stay home or join her family for Christmas. It hadn't felt right; how could she celebrate Christmas with someone else's family when she didn't even go home to see her own? So she avoided it altogether, except for calling her parents and sending them some gifts.

Other than that, Lydia avoided the holiday. She'd

had a lot of very happy Christmases growing up, and after what had happened with Ginny, she wasn't sure she deserved any more of them. But she was happy now—mostly, in moments. More than she had been in a long time.

She was also relieved to know that the tension she had detected from Ely earlier in the day had to be due to his thoughts about leaving the bodyguard business. She wondered about what other things he was thinking, but he hadn't seemed to want to talk. She hadn't pushed, and she questioned whether or not he trusted her enough to confide in her.

She stopped that train of thought, not liking how it made her feel. They were having a wonderful day, and she wasn't going to ruin it.

"Where are you going? The highway ramp is behind us," she said, perking up and noticing that they were heading back into the city instead of out of town. "I told you to use the GPS."

Ely chuckled. "I thought we might grab some dinner. I don't know about you, but that shopping left me starving."

"You're right. I wasn't even paying attention to the time," she said, looking at her watch. As if on cue, her stomach grumbled. Loudly.

Ely grinned. "I'll take that as agreement. What's your pleasure?"

"I think you have a pretty good idea of what I like," she said, unable to resist the tease. She *was* hungry— in more ways than one.

"That I do," he said in a low, promising voice that made her toes warm. "You like Middle Eastern food?"

"I like pretty much all food," she said. "But yeah,

that would be fun, if there is any. This isn't Philly," she joked.

He pulled into the lot of a small Middle Eastern restaurant a few minutes later, to her surprise, almost as if he had known exactly where to go. She looked at him with narrowed eyes.

He shrugged. "I spotted it on the way through town the first time."

"So many new places have sprung up—it's much more diverse and cosmopolitan than it was when I was here. People were too conservative to want much other than steakhouses and chain restaurants then," she said as they walked in. "This place looks new, and amazing. We might have needed reservations, though." There were a ton of cars parked out front. It seemed very busy. A positive sign that the food was good, but a bad sign for getting a table.

"I'll talk to the hostess, no worries," Ely said confidently, and sure enough, they were being led to a very nicely positioned table a few minutes later.

A small, low stage was only a few yards away, their view unobstructed.

"Wow, this is great seating for just walking in—the place is packed," she said, glancing around.

"I guess it was just meant to be," Ely said lightly, scanning the menu.

Something in his tone and how he didn't meet her eyes made Lydia pause, but then she shrugged and studied the menu. Ely ordered some wine and appetizers, and they both chose their entres.

"That's going to be a lot of food," she said, chagrined. "And I noticed baklava on the dessert menu— can't pass that up."

"We can take any leftovers with us for a treat later,"

he said, pouring the white wine just as the stage lit and a woman walked out in silence, bowing to the crowd. They didn't clap, but made a vocal sound of appreciation Lydia knew was called *zaghareet*. She and Ely joined in, and then everyone quieted as the dance began.

The music was sensual, the low beat traveling through the floor where Lydia could feel it up through the soles of her boots, and she glanced at Ely, who captured her hand on top of the table as they watched. His thumb rubbed her skin in a rhythm that matched the beat of the dance as the woman gracefully bent and swayed in almost impossible ways.

Then, to Lydia's amazement, the dancer moved to the edge of the stage and picked up a sword, balancing it on the top of her head as she danced, and then on her forehead as she bent to the floor, laying back in a deep backbend, her hips and arms moving as her torso and head stayed still.

It was one of the most wonderful dances Lydia had ever seen. Ely agreed, she thought, his hand tightening on hers just slightly. She noticed he had stopped watching the dance, though, and was watching her. She didn't mind at all. Ely might seem like a white-bread kind of guy, she thought, but he loved things that were exotic and different. Perhaps from his time in other countries, she mused.

"The sword dance is traditional in a lot of Middle Eastern and African countries," Ely leaned in and whispered. "It's a symbol of her reverence for her husband or lover's masculinity and honor. The dance with the sword and the care she takes with it is a symbol of her devotion to him," he said.

"It's beyond amazing how she can do that," Lydia agreed, but was also impressed with his knowledge.

Lydia made a silent New Year's resolution to look up some local belly dancing instruction when she got back to Philly. Maybe she could get Tessa to go along, as well.

Their appetizers arrived when the dance ended, and they ate for a little while, appreciating the savory fare of olives, hummus and spicy lamb kabobs. But the more they watched each other, and touched each other, the less important dinner became than being alone. Lydia met Ely's eyes, speculating how on earth they could make it through this meal and back to the ranch before they would give in and rip each other's clothes off.

"Maybe we should take this to go," she suggested none too subtly.

"Let's enjoy it. We have time," he said mysteriously.

And so they did, feeding each other bits from all of the plates. Ely fed her some of his with his fingers, letting them touch her lips incidentally, and Lydia was almost dizzy with need by the time she finished the sensual, slow meal.

They ordered desert and Ely asked the server to pack it up with their leftovers, obviously ready to go now, too. Once he paid, he headed to the door, her hand in his as he led the way. She wanted out, to get somewhere alone—and fast—where they could be alone to work off some of the heat.

Even the cold blast of air as they emerged from the restaurant didn't dampen their arousal. They were barely inside the car when she crawled over to straddle him in the driver's seat, kissing him with all of the desire that had built over the dinner.

"I don't think I have ever needed anyone so much," she said against his mouth, her breath coming in hard pants that steamed up the windows. "I can't wait until we get back."

He murmured agreement, his hands underneath her coat, holding her bottom and rubbing her where he was hard until she cried out.

"Unzip," she said, moving to give him some room.

"Not here," he said, his voice rough.

They stilled as voices rang outside the car, a group leaving the restaurant.

"Ely, it's an hour back to the ranch, at least," Lydia objected. "I want you now."

"I want you, too, but we don't have to wait that long," he said, pushing her back into the passenger seat and starting the car.

"What do you mean?" she asked.

"I reserved a room. It's just down the street," he said, looking at her as the fogged windshield cleared.

"You got us a room? When?"

"As soon as I knew we were coming into town. I thought we could both use a break. Some private time."

Light dawned and she nodded. "Ah. You had reservations at that restaurant, too, didn't you?"

"Guilty as charged," he said, putting the car into gear and pulling out of the lot. A few minutes later they were at the Crown Plaza.

"C'mon," he said, running around to open her door and help her out, practically throwing the keys at the valet as they both laughed, hurrying into the lobby of the hotel.

Minutes later, they were in an elevator that was taking them up to what she thought she'd heard the clerk describe not as a room, but a *suite*. As she started to ask questions about that, Ely pressed her against the wall of the elevator and kissed any objections or worries away, reminding her of why they were here in the first place.

"Let me do this for you, Lydia. For us. Consider it

an early Christmas gift," he said against her ear, making shivers work up and down her spine.

No one had ever done anything like this for her before, and she wanted to object, but the idea of being alone, here, with Ely, for the whole night was too much temptation.

"But I didn't get you anything," she said with a smile, looking up into his eyes, relenting.

He grinned. "Sweetheart, you are more than gift enough," he said as the doors opened.

Lydia couldn't help but laugh as he stopped every three feet all the way to their room to kiss her senseless. He removed some piece of her exterior clothing—her hat, coat, gloves, scarf—so that by the time they reached the door of the suite, Lydia didn't care about anything except him taking the rest of it off, which was clearly his plan, too.

12

LYDIA WALKED IN ahead of Ely; he turned on the lights and she stood and took it in.

"Wow," she said. "I've never stayed in a suite before. This is so cool," she exclaimed, running to the window and taking in the view. The window of the main room looked down over the city, all of the twinkling city lights and Christmas lights blending in together.

"It was the only room they had available on short notice, but I figured why not enjoy our night in style," Ely said. He draped his coat over a chair and walked up behind her, sliding his hands around her and setting his chin on her shoulder. "There's a hot tub," he said, a mischievous grin reflecting back to her in the window's surface.

She turned in his arms, looking up into his face. "Thank you. This is a lovely idea," she said, pushing up on her tiptoes to kiss him lightly. But that only lasted a second before he took control and deepened the kiss to a purely carnal exploration that had her moaning against him.

Ely put his hands under her backside, pulling her up

as she wrapped her arms around his broad shoulders and her legs around his hips. Holding her with one arm while not breaking the kiss, he drew the curtains with his free hand and walked them back to the large sofa positioned in front of a flat-screen TV.

Settling back into the deep cushions, Lydia enjoyed the luxury of being able to take as much time as she wanted to explore Ely with no worries about anything outside of the room. This was their world, as far as she was concerned, and she planned to take advantage of every second of it.

Unwinding her arms and her legs and straddling him more comfortably, she slid her hands down and under the edge of his sweater, tugging it up over his head. He did the same for her, his eyes traveling over her face, then lower, reflecting his appreciation for the lacy bra and what it revealed.

"You're so beautiful it blows my mind," he said on a breath that made her catch her own. She leaned back, drawing her hands up her stomach, over her breasts and through her hair, letting her head fall back. He liked it when she put on a little show for him, and the hardening she felt beneath her bottom confirmed that.

Grinding against him in imitation of the belly dancer's moves, Lydia smiled as he groaned.

"Feels good to me, too. I want this to last," she said.

For all of their frantic rush from the restaurant, suddenly she wanted to take things as slow as humanly possible, drawing out every bit of pleasure she could from this night.

Biting her lip, she had an idea and wondered if Ely would go along. Sliding from his lap, she grabbed the remote control and sat back beside him.

"You want to watch television?" he asked incredulously. "With a perfectly good hot tub in the other room?"

"Not exactly," she responded, grinning. "Hot tub later," she said, clicking through the hotel menu options to the adult viewing schedule. She slid a look his way as the titles popped up on the screen.

"You into this, or will it turn you off?" she asked honestly. She didn't watch adult movies as a habit, but she didn't mind one now and then, depending on the situation. She had no idea of Ely's tastes.

"Can't say I watch too many, but I'm open to it," he said, watching her curiously.

"You choose," she said, handing him the remote and holding her breath in anticipation, wondering what he would choose. What secret fantasies would Ely reveal?

Lydia went to turn the lights off, allowing the glow of the TV to be the only lighting. He chose a film, and as it started, she stood in front of the screen. She took off her jeans and boots, leaving only her bra and panties on. Ely slid out of his clothes as well, welcoming her back to the sofa and into his arms where she curled up against his warm body, every nerve ending in her body hyperaware as the movie started.

The opening screen homed in on a beach sunrise, where a man sat alone on the beach, naked, and looking out at the water expectantly. His hand lowered and he started to pleasure himself, focusing on the water.

"Do it," Lydia whispered into Ely's ear, a little breathless, wondering if he would.

Pausing for a second, he shucked his shorts and took his cock in his hand, watching her rather than the screen as he made himself hard, stroking until Lydia sighed. He was gorgeous, and she loved watching him.

She turned back to the screen. "Oh, look. That's who he was waiting for."

"A mermaid?" he said with a chuckle.

"Hey, to each their own," Lydia joked and rubbed her hand over the muscles of his chest. They watched the mermaid magically form two gorgeous legs from her tail as she emerged out of the water, also completely naked, of course.

The woman from the sea didn't wait long to join her friend in the sand, falling down to his side and looking at him meaningfully as she stroked him and then took him fully with her mouth.

Replacing Ely's hand with her own, Lydia did the same, wrapping her fingers around him, and then sliding down to taste him as fully as the mermaid was doing for her lover.

"Oh, Lydia," Ely said thickly.

The man on the screen pulled away, and brought the mermaid up for a deep kiss, and Ely, keen to the game Lydia was playing now, did the same.

Lydia was so hot she thought she might melt as Ely's hands worked over her body. She was starting to have a very hard time keeping track of the movie.

Ely moved to kiss her shoulder, looking at the screen. "I think we might have a harder time with this part," he said, his tone husky with arousal and laughter.

Lydia turned to find several more mermaids emerging from the water, joining in the fun.

"Yeah, that could be difficult," she agreed, kissing him again, their own sighs and moans mingling with those on the TV.

He was hard as steel under her, his breath hot on her skin.

The need for Ely was merging with the sounds of ecstasy from the movie as she recited what was happening on screen. It pushed them both to an erotic peak that had her buckling into an orgasm almost as soon as he thrust inside. He followed quickly, pushing her over one more time before they both collapsed into each other.

The movie folks were still going at it; the man on the beach was being swarmed by horny mermaids. She and Ely couldn't help but laugh as they caught their breath, clicking the movie off.

"Do you do this often, I mean, watching these kinds of films?" he asked, finally catching his breath.

She snuggled down beside him. "Sex has always been fun for me, and I don't mind experimenting, as you know."

"It's one of the things that draws me to you, how different you are. Uninhibited. I like it. A lot," he said warmly, looking down at her.

Something clenched in her chest at the way he looked at her, something more than sex hiding behind his words. She smiled, moving away, putting just a little distance between them.

"Good, because it's still early," she said with a wicked grin. "And there is that hot tub you keep talking about."

An emotion she couldn't quite identify flickered in his eyes so quickly she thought that she might have imagined it, but then he smiled, too, reaching for her.

Lydia followed and tried not to think about how much she loved his laugh, the way he looked at her and the way he touched her, because pretty soon, it would be time to return to Philly, and to her normal life. And that plan didn't include Ely as anything other than a casual friend.

Still, as he hauled her close and held her tight, his kiss swamping any more thinking or conversation, she couldn't remember the last time any of her "friends" had made her feel exactly like this. There was definitely nothing casual about it.

ELY LAY IN THE huge bed wide awake, staring at the ceiling where a sliver of light snuck through the drawn curtains; Lydia was sleeping soundly next to him, curled up on her side of the bed. The hot tub still hissed and burbled over in the corner of the room, and he smiled, remembering what had happened there a few hours ago.

In spite of the intermittent insomnia he always experienced, he should be out like a light, too. Still, even as his desire for Lydia had consumed him for hours as they played out a number of fantasies and scenarios, once the passion passed, his mind was left ticking away thoughts like the clock on the bed stand.

Sex has always been fun for me, she'd said.

And sex with Lydia *was* fun. Ely was having a whole lot of fun, no doubt about that, but it was something else that had him awake and unsettled. Like how she moved away any time things became too intimate or how she closed him out when a conversation became too personal.

He'd known the deal going in—friends, albeit with benefits—only, but he wasn't even sure he felt like they were developing a friendship. Didn't friends share, trust, and rely on each other? Here, he was lying to her, although for her safety, and she was keeping a safe distance from him emotionally. The only two times she had really connected with him that way was when she told him about Ginny, and when she'd cried over her mother, by the tree.

It was as if the only connection they had was sexual, and Ely wanted…more. Not living together forever

and walking down the aisle—no white picket fences—
but he wanted to be something more to her than "fun."

Was he already starting to bore her? Was it inevi-
table, given her broader sexual experience? Maybe so.
For him, he felt as if he had only scratched the surface,
but he could see the end in her eyes. Lydia was already
mentally packing up her bags and leaving. The thing
was that he was leaving, too—they were going back to
Philly together. Did this have to be over? Did it have to
be one thing or the other?

Even now, she slept soundly, facing him, with him,
but apart. She'd crept over to her own side of the bed
and passed out, retreating back to her own space even
in sleep.

Ely closed the distance, moving his hand over her
shoulder, loving the smoothness of her skin, the strength
of her body underneath the softness. He traced the line
of one of her tattoos from her upper arm, down over
her collarbone to the slope of her breast. The nub at
the peak, soft in sleep, hardened as soon as he touched
it. Her soft sigh triggered a deep need inside of him to
touch her more, to have her close.

Right now, he couldn't imagine ever not wanting her.
Or at least, not for a very long time.

Easing downward, he replaced his hand with his
mouth, sucking gently on one tip then the other, his
hand traveling down to slide between her legs. She
moaned, still not quite awake, but her silky thighs
opened for him.

Her soft sounds and warmth invited him in. He
kissed her belly, her hip, and then explored that sweet,
slick spot that made her whimper his name on a sigh
of pleasure. It thrilled him to do that. More so than it
ever had before, with anyone else. Having Lydia open

to him, trusting him and wanting him, was more of a rush than he could say, even if it was only physical.

But soft in half sleep, she was irresistible. He grabbed a condom, his last one he realized, and did the one thing they hadn't done in all of their times together. Maybe this old-fashioned, face-to-face loving would seem quaint to her, but he wanted it. Levering over her, he lay down between her thighs, not entering her, but simply laying there, surrounded in her warmth.

"Ely," she whispered sleepily, her hand coming to his face. He kissed it, wanting something tender and gentle between them. Wanting her close when he was inside her.

"You awake?" he asked, nibbling at her earlobe.

"Mostly," she said, sighing. "What are you doing?"

He chuckled softly, nudging her with his erection. "I wanted you again," he said.

"Oh, that's nice," she responded with a smile, and tipped her face up to kiss him, starting to move from under him.

He stopped her. "No, this way…just like this," he said.

She stilled, and then relaxed, her arms coming around his shoulders.

"Okay," she agreed.

While the kink and the fun were great, for one moment, he wanted something quiet and real with Lydia.

"Okay," he echoed and leaned in to kiss her.

He didn't plunder or let the moment become frantic, but kept it slow and gentle, kissing and touching as he eased inside and slipped his hand down below her hip to gain some purchase.

She whimpered approvingly and wrapped her legs around his lower back, deepening the connection.

Blood pounded in Ely's brain, urging him to go faster, harder, to possess and take what was his, but he didn't give in to that, preferring instead to maintain the soft, steady glide that had his entire body shaking— and hers, too—as they made a very slow, lovely climb together.

She was clinging to him and crying out when she came. Kissing her deeply so that their connection was complete, he thrust again, finding his own release and not letting go or moving even several minutes after it passed.

It was what he needed. It felt…right. And he didn't want to move, to break the connection.

"Ely," Lydia said, her hands on his shoulders. "Did you fall back asleep?" she asked, a touch of humor in her tone.

She did that, too—used humor as one of her ways to avoid emotion and intimacy. It could be something that brought them closer, but Lydia used it to defuse instead. He still didn't move but pushed up on his arms, sliding his hands into her hair and taking a few more kisses before he responded.

"No, I just like being here, like this, with you."

"Oh," she said, and he didn't know if he detected a bit of apprehension in her tone. Her legs loosened from around him, letting him go. "I have to get up, though, sorry," she said with a slight chuckle, breaking the spell.

He nodded with a sigh, planting one more kiss on her mouth and feeling the cool air rush between them even if the room was plenty warm enough. She slid from the bed, went to the bathroom without another word and closed the door. Ely dispensed of the condom and found his shorts. Walking to the window, and he stared out at dawn as it crept over the sleeping city.

"You coming back to bed?" she said from the bed-room doorway.

"I don't think so. Not tired," he replied, though on some level, he was exhausted. "You can, though. We have a few hours before we need to check out."

"Is something wrong?" she asked, but she stayed in the doorway.

He took a deep breath, dove in.

"I was just thinking," he said, turning to face her.

"About what?"

"Us."

She didn't say anything, but he noted how she im-mediately wrapped her arms around the front of her. She'd put on one of the thick terry-cloth robes from the bath, and was covered from neck to calf. He smiled. The thing dwarfed her. It was cuter than hell, but he figured she wouldn't like hearing that.

"Don't worry. I know we're not in this for keeps. No wedding bells or promise rings," he said. "But why does this have to stop now? We can be friends—like this—back home, too. We're adults, right? We can do whatever we want."

She pushed a hand through her hair, her most prom-inent nervous habit. "Why are you bringing this up now, Ely?"

"I don't know. I guess because I just thought of it. I like being with you, and I don't feel like ending this yet," he said bluntly, putting it out there. "I don't know why we have to set a deadline."

She inched into the room slowly.

"I like being with you, too, but things would be too complicated at home. Too hard to explain to people who know us that we're just jumping each other's bones. People would expect—"

"That's bull. We don't have to explain anything. It's nobody's business and I'm not in the habit of sharing my sex life with my family, or anyone else, anyway," he said, hoping to lighten the tone, but also to appeal to her sense of reason.

Her arguments were flimsy; there was no reason that they couldn't be together whenever they wanted, wherever they wanted.

Unless of course, she really was done. Bored. Ready to move on.

"It's not that easy," she said, sounding frustrated.

"It's exactly that easy," he countered, digging in.

She frowned. "I don't know what to say. I don't understand."

"I've told you what I want. Do you know what you want, Lydia?"

She stood, tense, clearly annoyed, and then her shoulders slumped as she looked at him, nodding.

"You're right. I want more of this. More of you," she said, stepping up and sliding her hands over the front of his chest. "Maybe we could get together now and then at home. As friends," she said, shrugging, as if to make it less than it was. He bridled at that, but knew not to push.

Ely's heart thundered under her touch. She just agreed, albeit apprehensively, to seeing each other when they returned to Philly. Her concession felt fragile, like gossamer between them. He didn't want to damage it. His hands came up to cover hers.

"Very special friends," he said, stepping in closer until their hands were trapped between them.

The corners of her lips tilted up slightly. "Yes, very special friends," she responded with an eye roll. This time the humor reached out, and he felt it warm him.

Ely relaxed, having won the battle, and that was

enough since there was no war. He and Lydia were still on the same page, generally speaking, but a new connection had been formed. It was a great, sexy, hot connection, he thought, as they kissed.

His hands pulled her in, traveling around to her back and kneading the tense muscles there. The discussion had really tightened her up, but Ely knew how to take care of that. Amazingly, he was ready for her again, or would be soon, and walked her back to the bedroom, disposing of the robe as they went. She fell back on the bed with a laugh, more relaxed. He loved seeing her this way.

"Roll over," he said and smiled as she wiggled her eyebrows at him before complying.

But Ely wasn't in any hurry. Settling up over her thighs, he started a back rub that massaged every knot from her neck and shoulders. As his hands drifted over her, he lost himself in touching and studying the ink on her back, studying the angle of her shoulder blade and the dimple at the base of her spine. She moaned and pushed her bottom up against his erection.

"Can't. Out of condoms," he said with deep, deep regret.

"S'ok, I'm protected," she urged.

She pushed her hips up again, and Ely slid back to his feet, his hands trembling slightly at the idea of being with her this way. Standing by the edge of the bed, he urged her back toward him as he parted her thighs and stepped in between. The first touch of her skin to his was so intense he sucked in a breath and paused, uncertain how long he could last. Only Lydia could have him this hot after having spent himself so many times in the hours before. He didn't know what it was about her, but he liked it.

"Please, Ely," she said, her hands curling into the sheets, and he couldn't deny her a second longer, sliding inside, deep and easy, with a long groan at how good it felt.

"You're so hot, so soft," he managed, pulling back, then forward, then thrusting in again, faster, harder. He took in the curve of her back, the sway of her hips, the exotic ink, and wanted this to last forever. This was perfection, he thought, watching her body shudder before he lost any control he thought he had.

It was more than an hour later that they finally admitted that they had to pack up and head back to the ranch. There was a lot to do before the festival and before they got ready to return to Philadelphia the week after Christmas.

Now, however, Ely felt lighter since he wasn't facing their return with that sense of finality that had been dogging him. He and Lydia would continue to see each other when they wanted to, casually, and eventually their interest would probably flame out and they would remain friends. It was all he could possibly ask for and all he wanted, he told himself as he looked at her in the car and hushed any objections his heart was making.

13

Lydia was as nervous as could be when she finally came downstairs after changing clothes three times before settling on the first outfit she had put on. Ely's approving gaze as it traveled over her in the formfitting black pants and bright red wool sweater confirmed she had made a good choice. The thermal underwear she had on beneath were less sexy, but as she would be out in the garage at her booth doing henna tats for the first night of the festival, she wanted to stay warm.

"You are one sexy elf, indeed," Ely said, looking good in his own dark jeans and black sweater, a red flannel collar peeking out from underneath his collar. "Why don't we go walk around for a little while, first, and take it all in? Get something to eat before you man your booth?"

Lydia swallowed and looked toward the kitchen. "I have some things in the fridge, here, if you're hungry."

Ely peered closer. "Why are you so nervous? This will be fun."

"Right. The thought of being publicly humiliated by

people who don't want me here is really something to look forward to."

"That's not going to happen."

"Or what if no one comes to my booth, or thinks the tattoos are stupid?"

"That won't happen, either. If it does, you can do me, and I'll get as many as it takes to get everyone else interested."

Lydia had to smile. She was being ridiculous, she knew. If Ginny or her family showed up, they probably would just ignore her, if they came at all. She just really didn't want a repeat of what happened in the grocery store, and she felt like a target, to some extent, sitting out there for all to see.

But as Ely said, that wasn't going to happen. No doubt Ginny had no interest in seeing her, and whoever was harassing her wouldn't do so in front of possibly hundreds of people.

"Okay, then, I'm ready," she said brightly, joining him at the door.

She stepped out onto the porch and paused, catching her breath.

"Oh, wow," she said, taking it all in for the first time. They had seen it in parts, putting it all together, but now…it was like the entire area around the house and the barns had been transformed into some magical winter wonderland. Lights glowed everywhere above their heads, strung along and between the buildings. The decorated trees glittered and danced in the slight breeze, stacks of gifts donated by everyone in town piled underneath—the night was perfect. The sky was clear and the air was crisp—cold, yes, but in that clean, fantastic way that made everything seem sharper and brighter. People were drifting in from the main road, being diverted to park in the frozen field off to the left, behind the barn where she and Ely had had their snowball fight. Some kids came running in, laughing and looking at everything; some others just stood in happy awe, like she was, admiring it.

"You helped make this happen, Lydia. Keep that in mind," Ely whispered in her ear, delivering a kiss to her cheek. "Come here, there's something else you need to see."

They spotted Geri and Faith by a tree near the entrance, decorated in gold and silver. There was a plaque set beside it, and Ely steered Lydia around to see.

She'd expected it was a welcome to the festival—and it was—with an honorary message about her mother, and a thank-you to Lydia as well, for hosting the festival. Her picture was on the placard, alongside her mother's, and below, the picture of them baking cookies, as well as the one of her mother hanging lights. Lydia stared at it for a long time, letting it all wash through her. She was afraid to say anything in case she made a complete fool of herself.

"Do you like it?" Faith asked, sounding worried. Lydia realized she had been standing there, silent, for several minutes, and a larger crowd had gathered. "We thought those pictures really showed the resemblance between you two."

"It's wonderful," Lydia managed, and turned with a smile and a hug for Faith and Geri. "Thank you so much."

"No, the thanks is all to you," Geri said with a wink. "Now, let's get this party started!"

Laughter rose and more people arrived. Hot chocolate and the scent of freshly fried doughnuts as well as other treats filled the air, and the local school choruses took turns caroling as everyone went through the various booths and activities provided.

Lydia was so busy at her booth that she barely had time to look up—every teenager and tween in town, along with some of the adults—had lined up for her henna tats, and she just hoped she had enough supplies.

Ely brought her snacks and drinks, and she visited as she inked little paisley stars and other stylized Christmas decor on hands and forearms.

She was having such a great time, her nervousness evaporated quickly. She met some people she had known from before, people who spoke so nicely of her mother, and new people who had just moved here. Everyone was lovely.

"C'mon, time for a break," Ely interjected after about two hours. The festival went until eleven, which meant she had two hours left. Then she would do it again tomorrow night—now it was something she looked forward to.

"I don't need a break," she objected. "This is fun."

Turning around, Ely looked at the line of expectant customers and smiled. "Okay, she'll be right with you folks, just a minute," he said, dipping down and kissing her hard and long in front of everyone.

Lydia, shocked, had no response but to respond, aware of the chorus of *"oooooooo"* and the childish giggles from the younger kids.

"Sorry. *I* needed that," Ely said with a grin and a wink, and strode off looking like…well, like he had just kissed her in front of God and everyone.

"That looked like fun. I hope you don't mind that I cut to the front of the line," someone said, and Lydia looked away from Ely to find Ginny facing her.

Lydia froze, unsure what to say. "Of course not. Welcome," she murmured. But then she had no clue what would happen next.

"Listen, could we talk for a second?" Ginny asked, and Lydia agreed, a lump in her throat.

"I'll be back in ten, guys. Remember your spot in line and help yourself to some hot cocoa and cookies," she said with a too-bright smile as she invited Ginny farther in.

"I don't know what to say," Lydia said, unsure what else to say, and then took a breath. "No, I do know what to say. I'm sorry. I am so sorry, Ginny. I've said that a million times over the last twelve years, but never to you, and I should have done that. I never should have goaded you into riding that horse, and I am completely responsible for everything that happened that day. I wish I could change it, but I can't. I don't blame you for hating me. I hate myself for what I did. But I am sorry," Lydia said, meeting her former friend's eyes squarely.

Ginny looked gorgeous. Wrapped in a white wool coat and hat, her chestnut hair was gleaming, her cheeks pink, and her big brown eyes took in Lydia with stark surprise.

"Wow, that was quite a speech," Ginny said. "My turn now?"

Lydia braced herself for whatever Ginny had to say, and nodded. "Whatever you have to say to me, I know I deserve it."

"I'm sorry, too," Ginny said with a heavy breath, and Lydia just stared, confused.

"Sorry for what? What on earth are you talking about?"

Lydia watched as Ginny's hands clutched tightly in her lap.

"Well, I won't say that I didn't hate you after it happened. I was scared and I felt like everything I wanted was gone—including my best friend, who just…left. How could you go, Lydia? If ever I needed you, it was then."

Lydia was flattened. "But I…it was my fault…and your mother. I had to leave. It was best for everyone."

Ginny shook her head. "It wasn't best for me. I needed you. That's what I was angry with you about. For leaving. I know what my father said to you—but he was just distraught, as well. When you really left, well, everyone was stunned. What happened wasn't your fault—not entirely—believe me, several years of therapy taught me that. I'm the one who climbed up on that horse. That was my choice. But we were all kids. We did foolish things."

Lydia reeled, Ely's words coming back to her.

"Leaving was your choice, and I did hate you for that. But then your mother told me about you, what you were doing, the good and the bad, and she knew that you blamed yourself. That you refused to let yourself be happy. She gave me your number years ago. I know she hoped that we'd make contact again, and that maybe I could get you to come back," Ginny said, shaking her head and turning away.

"I didn't call because I thought that you might not want to come back here, be friends with me. That I was somehow repulsive to you. It's what I thought when we met in the store—you seemed so…horrified," Ginny said lamely, holding up her hand against Lydia's protest. "But your mother was sick, and she's gone now. And if I had called that number, you might have had more time with her. I suppose I feel that you didn't have that time because of me," Ginny said, her voice choking. "So for that, *I'm* sorry."

Lydia was beyond overwhelmed, trying to process it all, but her mind was spinning. How could things have been so terribly misunderstood, all of that time together—with Ginny, and her family—so tragically lost?

But Lydia pulled herself from the past to the present. There was nothing she could do about what had happened; but she could do something about right now.

"I'm not repulsed by you, Ginny. I wasn't then, and I'm not now. You're beautiful, brave…you always were. I just didn't think you'd ever want me around again. I was horrified in the store, for having to face up to my past and the consequences of what I'd done—not by you," Lydia said, trying to find words for it all. "I did see Mom before she died, and we talked, on the phone, and by email, over the years. Dad, too. Like you said, that was my choice, too, not coming home. Not your fault," Lydia said, sitting down hard on a bench by the wall.

"All that time wasted," Ginny said regretfully.

"Yeah," Lydia echoed, and they sat in silence for a moment.

"I loved the tattoo you gave my daughter. She couldn't wait to show me. I was wondering if I could have one to match it?"

Lydia's head snapped up. "Your daughter?"

Ginny grinned. "The second to last one you did. She's my youngest, of four."

"Four? You have four kids, but…"

"Medicine has come a long way," Ginny said with a smile. "I live a more or less normal life. And Charles is…really hot."

Lydia laughed, and then they were both laughing.

"Yeah, he is," Lydia agreed. "I could definitely do a tat for you to match your daughter's."

As she looked at Ginny and felt the weight fall away, Lydia was quite sure of a lot of things. She knew her mother wanted this above all else—for her to stop punishing herself for the past—and she couldn't let regrets hold her back any longer.

Giving in to the moment, she rushed forward and grabbed Ginny in a tight hug. For a second, it was like they were girls again, with all of their hopes and dreams ahead of them.

"Will you have some time after, or before you go back? To catch up?"

"I'll make time. I'd like nothing more," Lydia said.

"I'd better open the booth again, or there might be a revolt," Lydia said with a grin, releasing her friend. "But first, I think I need to do something."

Ginny smiled knowingly. "Something with your sexy new friend?"

Lydia couldn't stop the answering grin if she tried. "Yeah. I've been running away from everything, including him, and I want to let him know I'm not going to do that anymore."

"Good call. He's the kind of guy you want to let catch you, from what I've seen."

"He really is."

Though doubt must have shown in her face, as Ginny's hand reached out to give her arm a squeeze.

"Just let him know what you want. The rest will fall into place as it's supposed to," Ginny said wisely, and Lydia nodded, taking a bolstering breath.

"Let everyone know I'll be back in a bit, and that you're first in line," Lydia said with a grin, heading out the door.

She dashed in between the barns, and the alleys, but there were so many people it was hard to find Ely in the crowd. Then she noticed a light on up in the bedroom of the house, and smiled.

Maybe they would be taking a little break after all.

14

LYDIA CLIMBED THE stairs, relieved to be out of the rush of the festival and eager to have a few minutes alone with Ely. Nerves were rattling inside her gut, but she was determined to do this before she let any reservations keep her from saying what she had to say.

"Ely, hey, I need to—" Lydia said, entering but stopping short, finding not Ely, but Kyle in her bedroom.

He paused, looking up from a knapsack he was filling with something. Money, she realized, her eyes focused on the fat wad of bills in his hand.

"What are you doing? What's that?" she asked, trying to process what she was seeing.

Kyle sighed, glaring at her as if she was a nasty bug he wanted to squash.

"It's my retirement, and you're supposed to be busy outside with the festival."

"But where…how…?"

"None of your damned business. Where's loverboy? Meeting you up here for a little slap and tickle?" he asked, sneering.

He reached into the bag before she could answer, drawing out a gun.

"Kyle," she said, backing up and putting her hands up defensively. "I don't know what this is, but I'm not going to stop you. Just go. Don't hurt anyone," she said, her heart hammering.

"That's how it would have been if you hadn't come snooping."

Snooping? In her own house?

"Come here," he ordered, waving the gun.

She paused, and he asked again, more emphatically, so she did.

"Finish packing this, while I keep an eye out. Then we'll take a nice friendly stroll down to my truck, and you can go back to your life."

Lydia wondered if he really meant it, but did as she was told, trying to think frantically about how she could signal someone, anyone, from the window, but there was no way.

She looked down at the bottom of the guest room closet to find the boards pulled up, the remainder of a large stash of money still hidden inside. She reached down and grabbed two handfuls.

"How long has this been hidden here?"

"I have no idea. I've been searching for their stash for over a month. I've been through every abandoned property and building for five miles, and this was the only place left," Kyle said in agitation. "I figured it had to be in the house. I had found it the other day when your boyfriend conveniently agreed to get you out of the house for the night, but then Smitty was hanging around late with some of the festival guys, and I couldn't get it out without someone noticing. I thought tonight would be the perfect distraction, but you've been messing this up from the start."

Everything clicked in her brain as she packed more of the money into the bag.

"Gee, so sorry," she said sarcastically. "You were in the truck…you've been harassing me."

"I had another guy helping out, you know, just to throw you off the scent, but you don't scare easily, do you, Lydia?" He looked at her with something between admiration and lust, and she broke eye contact, shuddering.

"We'll be gone in a week or so. Why not just wait?" she asked.

"The money would be gone then, too—the guys who are coming up from South America for it wouldn't think twice about putting a bullet in your head to get you out of their way, so consider this your lucky break."

"So this isn't yours?"

"It is now," he said with a laugh, and then was quiet as he watched her pack up the rest and zip the bag. "About time I got some payoff for dealing with these sleazebags all these years."

Lydia stared. "You're a cop?" she asked incredulously.

"Fed, actually. Been undercover here for a while, and when this opportunity came up, I decided it was time."

Lydia hoped that if Kyle really was a cop, he would be less inclined to kill her—or maybe it made him more dangerous.

"What do you mean Ely agreed to get me out of town? He'd never agree to help you."

"He thought he was helping me for his D.C. buddies. When he got involved, I knew I had to move fast."

Lydia digested that. So Ely had known about Kyle,

and he hadn't told her? And their entire night together in Billings had been arranged so that Kyle could search her house?

She couldn't focus on that now, and Kyle seemed done with the conversation, too, as he hauled her up by the arm, closing the closet door.

"Okay. Now we walk down to my truck, nice and easy. I'll have to tie you up so you can't go run and alert anyone too soon, and then I'll be gone. If you decide to mess with me, or alert anyone, especially your boyfriend or the sheriff, people will get hurt, do you understand?" he asked, jamming the gun into the small of her back.

"Okay, yeah," she said, holding her breath and walking out of the room, her mind spinning.

What if Kyle didn't keep his word? What if he killed her, and she never got to tell Ely how she felt, or that she wanted to be with him as more than his casual sex partner? To see if they had a future? To find out if he was even interested in a future, she thought, her mind going back to what Kyle had said.

Maybe she really was just a temporary fling to Ely.

She wouldn't cause Kyle to hurt anyone, especially Ely, or any of the kids running around the festival grounds. She was trapped, she thought as they exited through the back door. Kyle had his arm slung around her in a friendly way as they emerged into the crowd, his other hand holding the gun at her side.

"Just make like we're two pals, enjoying the festivities."

"People will miss me at the booth."

"They'll find you when they come looking."

Find her how, exactly, she thought, a chill taking over that had nothing to do with the cold.

Out of the corner of her eye she saw Faith, in Steve Granger's arms, looking like perhaps they had mended a few fences of their own. Lydia wondered if she would ever feel Ely's arms around her again.

A few people said hello, and paused to thank her for such a great time, and she smiled briefly, trying not to sound unnatural as she acknowledged their sentiment and kept walking. Kyle was getting nervous, she could tell, the gun poking harder into her side.

It only took a minute or two to reach the bunkhouse down past the festival area. They were alone.

At least, even if the worst happened, she'd kept him from hurting anyone else. It was a comfort.

Kyle dragged her to the storage shed beside the bunkhouse and opened the door. Lydia heard mumbling. Looking into the small, cold space, she saw Roger—Faith's nephew—also bound and bleeding from his temple. He was shivering visibly, his eyes bleary.

"What did you do?" Lydia hissed, turning on Kyle. "Why are you picking on a kid?"

"Watch it," he said, grabbing her roughly and jerking her arm behind her back, pushing her into the shed where she stumbled and fell down beside Roger. "Roger was my little helper, and I was compensating him nicely for it, until he decided he might rat," Kyle said, grabbing a rag from his pocket that he intended to stuff into her mouth, as he had done with Roger.

"Roger was the one helping you harass me? To get me out of the house?"

"Yeah, until I caught him heading for the sheriff's office this morning. Caught him just in time," Kyle said. "Grab a few of those plastic ties there on the shelf—do your ankles, then your hands—behind your back. Good," he approved her application of the ties and shoved the gun back into his belt, stepping forward with the gag. "Now this will keep you quiet until I'm long gone."

Lydia caught a glint of something out of her eye—someone behind Kyle? She wasn't sure.

"So who hid the money?"

"One of the cartel's local guys. I saw him leaving here one day, and started searching, but never could find it. Then you showed up back in town and began digging through everything."

"The people who come after that money are going to know it's missing, and they'll come after you," she tried desperately to keep him talking, keep him there.

"That's the best part. They'll figure you took it, or the kid, or your boyfriend," he said with a laugh. "And they'll never find me, honey, because I don't exist. I'd watch your back from here on in, if I were you."

"I think you should do the same," she said, smiling as she saw Ely appear behind Kyle in the doorway of the shed, shotgun in hand.

"Yeah, right. Now open wide," he said maliciously, intending to gag her with an old rag.

"Touch her again and I'll drop you where you stand," Ely said dangerously, and Kyle froze.

"Ely, he has a gun," she said as Kyle tried to reach for his weapon, but Ely closed in and hit Kyle hard in the back of the head with the butt of the gun before the man could do anything.

Steve Granger turned the corner just then, his expression dangerous, his gun drawn, as well. He looked at Kyle moaning on the floor of the shed, and holstered his weapon. Taking in Lydia and Roger as Ely disarmed Kyle and gave the forty-five to Steve, the sheriff smirked.

"Well, hell, I thought I told you to wait," he said to Ely.

"Things move fast, Granger. And I really, really wanted to hit this guy," Ely said, working on Lydia's and Roger's restraints as Granger cuffed Kyle and called for an ambulance.

Within minutes chaos broke out around them, but all Lydia cared about was being in Ely's arms. She was safe now. People buzzed all around her as the police shut down the festival early and cleared out the crowd, but Lydia hardly noticed.

She couldn't seem to stop touching Ely as the police took her report, and the EMTs took Roger off to the hospital. He would be okay, but had come dangerously close to hypothermia.

"How did you know?"

"We saw him go in the house. Steve and I were watching from the crowd, waiting for him to come out, but then you went in, and that changed everything."

"So you all knew?"

"I told Steve I found out that he was undercover DEA, and apparently Steve already knew—they were keeping an eye on him, worried that he was dirty. Turns out it was true. I had a feeling if he found something in the house, he was going to try to take off with it."

"Why didn't you tell me? How could you keep this all from me?" she asked, bewildered by what was happening right under her nose.

"I needed to play it close. I also couldn't risk Ian— Kyle—finding out. It would have put you in danger if he thought you knew. Even more so," he said.

He'd been protecting her. It was what he did—his job.

What she really wanted to know was if their night in Billings had just been part of the plan, as Kyle said, or if it had been as special as she thought it was. But that wasn't fair. She had set the terms of their relationship—keep it casual. She had told him that she didn't want commitment.

He had told her he was looking for a fresh start, new adventures, and nothing to tie him down. He hadn't come out here for her, but at Tessa's bidding. None of that had changed even though Lydia had a feeling that she had changed significantly.

She wanted all of those things—or at least, she was more open to the possibility, now that she didn't need to shut herself off from happiness anymore.

But that wasn't fair to Ely. At least they had decided that they would remain "friends" when they went back to Philly. Maybe in time…well, she could hope.

They walked into the house, alone, together, everything quiet again. The festival would reopen the next night, but for now, they could focus on each other, and the close call they'd had.

"He said Roger was helping him."

"Yeah. I knew the kid was involved somehow, but had no idea he was in that deep."

"I wonder what Steve will do? It looked like he and Faith were getting back together."

"Roger was grabbed by Kyle trying to go to Steve to tell him about the operation, and about you. That counts, and the kid paid a pretty severe price as it is. Hopefully he'll learn a lesson. I'm betting he doesn't charge him, or at the very least, Roger gets off on probation."

Lydia hoped that, as well.

Ely pulled her down into the deep couch with him, and Lydia snuggled in. She turned, looking up into his face, framing it with her hands. A warm, possessive feeling captured her, and if she never had to move from this spot, she'd be a happy woman.

So this was love? she wondered. Did it always sneak up quietly like this, happening all at once, or had it actually been there all along, and she'd been afraid to see it?

"What are you thinking?" Ely asked, studying her face.

"I'll tell you later," she said, worried that telling Ely about her newfound feelings would be too much and would ruin what they did have together. She couldn't just change the rules because her feelings had changed—could she?

Reaching up for a kiss, Lydia decided that she didn't really want to talk right now anyway. He started to say something, and she put a finger to his mouth. Standing, she took off her clothes and then did the same for him.

She straddled him, taking him in and moving with a gentle rocking of her hips. She felt more connected to him in that instant than she had to anyone in her life. Soon, they were both clinging to each other and gasping through their climax.

Wrapping her arms around his neck, she pressed against him, loving how it felt to be this close to him, their bodies still connected, his arms banded around her. She closed her eyes, sealing in tears that threatened from the emotion that overwhelmed her.

This was what they had, and it was what she had told him that she wanted. For now, it had to be enough.

A LITTLE LESS THAN a week later, Ely sat in front of the computer on Christmas Eve morning, scanning airline ticket prices. Several of them were good—not many people were traveling to Philly the week between Christmas and New Year's, but he couldn't settle on one.

The house had been more or less cleared out. The

festival was over—having gone off with booming success—and Lydia had made peace with her past. He'd enjoyed meeting her friends, seeing her happy, and now she was ready to get back to Philly and get on with her life.

Very likely without him, he realized suddenly.

He didn't want to go.

He didn't want to go back to Philly, back to his job, back to just being friends with Lydia, even if their friendship would have intimate benefits.

It had all been sneaking up on him, working on his imagination over the last few weeks. He loved this place. He loved the house, the ranch and the town. He loved the snow and the open spaces. The day before he'd found himself looking into the local university degrees in architecture, and he'd even been helping Smitty with the cows and horses all week, now that they were one man down.

He loved Lydia most of all.

They'd had a fantastic week together—the danger and anxiety gone, she was like a new person. Lighter, happier. Their lovemaking had become so much more than sex for him—and he knew she wouldn't want to hear that.

He hadn't lied to her, back at the start. He really thought he didn't want to be tied down; the truth was that he didn't know what he wanted. Until now.

But Lydia was packing to leave right after Christmas— the day after tomorrow. He'd heard her talking on the phone to Tessa, excited about going home.

Lydia had been right from the start. Ely wasn't built for temporary. He'd been hers from that first ill-advised night they'd shared to this moment, right now. And he'd be hers for a long time to come, he knew.

And she wouldn't want that.

Going back to Philly would be impossible. How could he go back and just be her "friend"? How could he watch her take other lovers?

He couldn't.

Suddenly he knew exactly what he needed to do.

Grabbing his phone, he made the call he'd been thinking about, the one that he'd known he would make weeks ago.

After that, he called Jonas and told him what he was doing. That he was staying. Jonas had been surprised, but supportive, as Ely knew he would be. He'd also been curious about what else had happened—perceptive, his brother—but Ely told him he didn't want to talk about it. Not now.

He stood, intending to go downstairs, bracing himself to tell Lydia, but then he turned around to find her in the doorway, watching him.

"I just got an offer on the ranch," she said, still carrying the phone in her hand. "I can't believe it. The Realtor just called and told me someone put in a bid for the asking price, not even bothering to negotiate lower. And they want it, lock, stock and barrel, the animals, all of it."

Ely smiled. "That's wonderful, sweetheart. Listen—"

This was what she wanted, and that made him happy; it also broke his heart, since he knew what was making her happy was going to take her away from him.

He crossed the room to pull her into his arms, and she hugged him back, but felt tense in his hold.

"What's wrong?" he asked.

She broke away, pushing her hands through her hair, the usual sign she was conflicted. Quiet for a moment, she moved in to face him.

"I know this sounds crazy, but I'm not going to sell," she said.

The news knocked him back a step.

"What? Why?"

She had a stranglehold on the phone with both hands, and he knew she was anxious about something. In fact, the smile she'd had when she announced the news had faded considerably.

"I can't go back to Philly."

"Why not? Is it something Tessa said? Was she angry over you not telling her—"

"No. We had a long talk, and she was completely understanding. I've underestimated people terribly— Ginny and Tessa—I was so sure they would hate me. But they've been nothing but wonderful."

"That happened because you were so angry with yourself."

"Well, not anymore. I need a fresh start, I think. And I think, for me and you, it would be better to have a clean break," she said. "I can't keep being friends with you, Ely. I'm sorry. I know I said differently when we were in the hotel, in Billings, but I don't think it would be for the best."

Realization set in for him. She couldn't go back because she didn't want things to be awkward or difficult with him. She wanted to move on.

He straightened his spine. "It's okay. Seeing me in Philly won't be a problem. I'm the one who put in the bid," he said, approaching her.

"What?" she blurted, staring at him in shock.

"On the ranch. I want to stay here. I've really come to love this place. I told you I was thinking about going part-time with my brothers, but now my cousin Luke is there, and he can take my place. Though I could go back if they really need me," he said, shrugging, knowing he was babbling. "But the point is that you don't have to worry about any awkwardness at home because of me—I'm going to stay here. If you accept the offer."

Lydia's shocked expression continued. "You're staying here?"

"Yeah."

"Because you love the ranch?"

"I do. I hope that gives you some comfort, to know that I'll have it. I'll take good care of it, and Smitty can stay on, too, of course."

"I don't understand…why? You can't make a huge decision like that out of thin air—"

"I can't go on being friends, either, Lydia. I know it was supposed to stay casual, but you were right. I didn't really change. I love this place, the land, the house, and I want to settle down. I love you, too."

She stared at him, speechless, and he knew it was probably the last thing she wanted to hear.

"It's okay. I know you need to go. And the sale from the place will help you open a new shop, like you wanted, so I hope you will accept."

"You love me?" she asked, staring into his face as if trying to see if it was true.

"I do. So much that I can't go back and just be your friend with benefits, and I know I can't watch you—"

He was cut off as she jumped into his arms. Wrapping her whole body around him as she kissed him, shutting him up, he was nearly thrown off of his feet.

Gaining his balance, he kissed her back for as long as she wanted to kiss him—he could never stop kissing Lydia—but then she broke the kiss and looked at him.

"I can't sell you the ranch, Ely," she said, shaking her head. His heart plummeted.

"Why not?"

"I thought instead I might put your name on the deed. It could belong to both of us. We could live here, and go back to Philly often, since I still have the shop there, which I want to keep. But I can find someone to run that one. I was thinking about taking over Dot's shop in Billings, and turning it into a Body Inc. here. And I'd have to be here for that," she said, her cheeks flushed, eyes bright.

Ely blinked, unsure he could trust what he was hearing.

"Wait. *We?* You want to stay here, too, with me?" The words were tight as Ely held his breath. "I thought you said you didn't want to be friends anymore?"

"I don't. I want to be more. Way, way more," she said, diving in for another kiss, but this time he stopped her.

"How much more?"

Several heartbeats passed between them before she looked him in the eye and said what he needed to hear.

"All of it. Everything. Whatever you want. House, kids, white picket fences. Well, maybe not those, but you know what I mean. I love you, too. That's why I couldn't go back. I couldn't stand just being friends, either. Not when I love you like crazy. I thought I had set the rules, and you didn't want more. So I couldn't just change my mind."

"Oh," he said, sounding shell-shocked.

"Yeah."

"I guess if we're going to share ownership of the house, we should probably share other things. You know, like my last name, maybe," he said tentatively, going for it.

"Yeah, I think you're right," she said, nibbling at his neck, arrows of heat darting through him with every touch of her mouth.

Carrying her over to the bed, Ely laid her down there, but stayed standing, undressing her and then himself as he looked at her, taking her in.

"So, you won't sell me the ranch, but you'll marry me, stay here with me, share everything with me, and build a life with me?"

"Absolutely," she said, then bit her lip as a tear escaped, and she cursed, swiping at it and making him chuckle.

That was his Lydia.

His.

All his.

Lowering down, he covered her and connected them as deeply as he could as the room darkened, more snow moving in. It was plenty warm inside, Ely thought as he lowered for another kiss.

"This is the best Christmas ever," Lydia whispered against his mouth.

Ely couldn't agree more.

Epilogue

CHANCE BERRINGER stretched in the big bed, rolling over to stare out at the snowy mountains outside his lodge window. A rustling of the sheets behind him reminded him that he had company.

He hadn't forgotten, exactly, but after a day of skiing, and then almost twenty-four hours straight at the hospital with his friend Logan after a serious accident, he was exhausted inside and out. When the pretty nurse on Logan's floor had been leaving for the night at the same time Chance was, he'd found he didn't want to be alone. Not after nearly losing one of his best friends.

Jenna—he still didn't know her last name—had been more than sympathetic, and happy to take care of him.

"Hey, you. Awake?" she asked, taking his attention away from the mountains as her hands traveled over his back, loosening any tension.

"Oh, that feels great," he groaned, pushing fully over onto his stomach and letting her massage every inch of his back. Except that his cock was getting hard against the mattress.

"Let me turn over and maybe you can do the front,"

he suggested. Jenna giggled, more than willing, allowing him to turn.

He approved when she leaned over to grab a condom and applied it with expert hands before lowering back over him.

This was what it was all about, he thought, watching her ride him, her mussed blond hair sliding forward over her shoulders as those perfect, ripe breasts pointed right at him, begging for a taste.

"You were just what the doctor ordered," he said, rising up to take a firm peach-toned nipple in between his teeth and biting lightly as he had discovered she enjoyed. That made her ride him harder, which he enjoyed, very much.

Just as she tightened around him, on the edge of climax and spilling over, the phone rang. Jenna pushed her hand hard against his chest as he reached for it, stopping him as she saw out her orgasm and then smiled down at him, breathless.

"Okay, you can answer it now," she said, laughing as she slid from the bed and walked to the shower. He shook his head, chuckling and admiring her brashness. She had a great walk, he noted as she crossed the room, and an ass a man could sink his teeth into, among other things.

Then he saw the name on his cell and his smile faded: Jillian.

Logan's wife. Chance's stomach sank. Had something happened to his friend?

"Jill, is everything okay?"

"Yeah, that's what I wanted to tell you. They took him off the life support this morning, and he's doing a lot better. He even talked to me a little. But he was really tired, and on the drugs, you know?"

Chance swung his legs over the side of the bed, staring back out at the mountain, at the ridge that had nearly killed his buddy.

"That's great news," he said, trying to sound cheerful, for Jillian's sake. "What can I do? Do you need me there?" he asked, standing and checking his watch, willing to do whatever his friends wanted.

"No, I'm fine, really. My parents and Logan's mom will be here today. Thanks for being there for us, Chance. I can't tell you what it means to me that you were with him, just in case, well, you know, but I think he's going to be okay. A long road ahead, but it will be okay. I hope you'll come see us once he's home again. The doctors said it might be a month or so, and then he'll have outpatient rehab. He'll need his friends around to get through it, I think. Me, too," she said, sounding on the verge of tears. Jill was one of the strongest women he knew, but this had wrecked her.

Chance swallowed hard, unable to stop the flashes of memory. Logan plummeting over the ridge. Logan lying in the snow like a broken children's toy. Logan in the hospital bed, hooked up to so many machines he didn't even look like himself.

"You won't be able to keep me away," he said warmly, and he meant it. He'd be there for them in any way that they needed him.

Hanging up, he listened to the shower running, but his previous ardor had evaporated. It had been good to work off some steam, and Jenna had helped him keep the recent memories of Logan's fall at bay so he could sleep.

Sudden restlessness gripped him; a need to get out. He recognized the feeling.

He'd paid for the room for two more days, but it was

time to leave. He wrote Jenna a note, letting her know she could use the room if she wanted—she'd mentioned having a few days off—and ordered some flowers to be delivered later. Meanwhile, he packed. She was a great girl, and he hoped she'd appreciate his gesture, because he wasn't stopping to say goodbye.

Ten minutes later, he was out the door, heading to the airport. He needed to get home, and he needed to get to work. His brothers had to have some jobs waiting, especially as they were short-handed now with Ely quitting to stay in Montana. To run a ranch, get married and study architecture. They had Luke on now, but he was more of a white-collar kind of guy. Chance was looking forward to seeing him, and now couldn't wait to get home.

Chance shook his head as he looked out the window of the cab. Well, to each their own. If anyone had earned a chance to live their dreams, it was Ely.

His brothers were all settling down, but he was just the opposite. He was young, healthy and ripe for his next adventure—and that was what he was going to find.

* * * * *

COMING NEXT MONTH FROM
HARLEQUIN® BLAZE™

Available December 18, 2012

#729 THE RISK-TAKER • *Uniformly Hot!*
by Kira Sinclair

Returned POW Gage Harper is no hero. He blames himself for his team's capture in Afghanistan, and the last thing he wants is to relive his story. But journalist Hope Rawlings, the girl he could never have, is willing to do anything to get it. Gage just might be her ticket out of Sweetheart, South Carolina—and what a hot ticket he is!

#730 LYING IN BED • *The Wrong Bed*
by Jo Leigh

Right bed...wrong woman. When FBI agent Ryan Vail goes undercover at a ritzy resort to investigate a financial scam at an intimacy retreat for couples, he'll have to call on all his skills. Like pretending to be in love with his "wife," aka fellow agent Angie Wolf. Problem is he and sexy Angie had a near fling months ago, and now the heat is definitely on while they share a hotel room—and a bed. Can they get through all those grueling intimacy exercises, all that touching and caressing...without giving the game away?

#731 HIS KIND OF TROUBLE • *The Berringers*
by Samantha Hunter

Bodyguard Chance Berringer must tame the feisty celebrity chef Ana Perez to protect her, but the heat between them is unstoppable, and so may be the danger.... Ana dismisses the threats at every turn, but she can't dismiss Chance or their incredible sexual chemistry. Soon the boundary between personal and professional is so blurred that Chance must make the hardest decision of all....

#732 ONE MORE KISS
by Katherine Garbera

When a whirlwind Vegas courtship goes bust, Alysse Dresden realizes she has to pick up the pieces and move on. Now, years later, her ex insists he'll win her back! Though she's curious about what's changed his mind, Alysse is reluctant to give her heart another chance, not to mention Jay Cutler. Still, she can't deny he's the one man she's never forgotten.

#733 RELENTLESS SEDUCTION
by Jillian Burns

A girls' weekend in New Orleans sounds like the breakout event Claire Brooks has been waiting for. But when her friend goes missing, Claire, who's always been on the straight and narrow, admits she needs the help of local Rafe Moreau, a mysterious loner. Rafe's raw sensuality tempts Claire like no other...and she can't say no!

#734 THE WEDDING FLING
by Meg Maguire

Tabloid-shy actress Leigh Bailey has always avoided scandal. But she's bound to make the front page when she escapes on a tropical honeymoon getaway—without her groom! Lucky her hunky pilot Will Burgess is there to make sure she doesn't get too lonely....

REQUEST YOUR FREE BOOKS!
2 FREE NOVELS PLUS 2 FREE GIFTS!

red-hot reads!

YES! Please send me 2 FREE Harlequin® Blaze™ novels and my 2 FREE gifts (gifts are worth about $10). After receiving them, if I don't wish to receive any more books, I can return the shipping statement marked "cancel." If I don't cancel, I will receive 6 brand-new novels every month and be billed just $4.49 per book in the U.S. or $4.96 per book in Canada. That's a saving of at least 14% off the cover price. It's quite a bargain. Shipping and handling is just 50¢ per book in the U.S. and 75¢ per book in Canada.* I understand that accepting the 2 free books and gifts places me under no obligation to buy anything. I can always return a shipment and cancel at any time. Even if I never buy another book, the two free books and gifts are mine to keep forever.

151/351 HDN FEQE

Name _____ (PLEASE PRINT)

Address _____ Apt. #

City _____ State/Prov. _____ Zip/Postal Code

Signature (if under 18, a parent or guardian must sign)

Mail to the **Reader Service:**
IN U.S.A.: P.O. Box 1867, Buffalo, NY 14240-1867
IN CANADA: P.O. Box 609, Fort Erie, Ontario L2A 5X3

Not valid for current subscribers to Harlequin Blaze books.

Want to try two free books from another line?
Call 1-800-873-8635 or visit www.ReaderService.com.

* Terms and prices subject to change without notice. Prices do not include applicable taxes. Sales tax applicable in N.Y. Canadian residents will be charged applicable taxes. Offer not valid in Quebec. This offer is limited to one order per household. All orders subject to credit approval. Credit or debit balances in a customer's account(s) may be offset by any other outstanding balance owed by or to the customer. Please allow 4 to 6 weeks for delivery. Offer available while quantities last.

Your Privacy—The Reader Service is committed to protecting your privacy. Our Privacy Policy is available online at www.ReaderService.com or upon request from the Reader Service.

We make a portion of our mailing list available to reputable third parties that offer products we believe may interest you. If you prefer that we not exchange your name with third parties, or if you wish to clarify or modify your communication preferences, please visit us at www.ReaderService.com/consumerschoice or write to us at Reader Service Preference Service, P.O. Box 9062, Buffalo, NY 14269. Include your complete name and address.

Bestselling Blaze author Jo Leigh
delivers a sizzling *The Wrong Bed* story with

Lying in Bed

Ryan woke to the bed dipping. For a few seconds, his adrenaline spiked until he remembered where he was. He groaned at the bright red numbers on the clock. "One a.m.? What…?"

The rest of the question got lost in the dark, but it didn't matter, because Jeannie didn't answer. His fellow agent on this sting must be exhausted after arriving late. "You okay?"

She tugged sharply on the covers, pulling more of them to her side of the bed.

Ryan could just make out her head on the pillow, her back to him, hunched and tight. Must have gotten stuck at the airport….

He curled onto his side, hoping to find the dream she'd interrupted. It had been nice. Smelled nice. He sighed as he let himself slip deeper and deeper into sleep…. The scent came back, a little like the beach and jasmine, low-key and sexy—

His eyes flew open. His heart thudded as his pulse raced. No need to panic. That was Jeannie next to him. Who else would it be?

Undercover jitters. It happened. Not to him, but he'd heard tales. Moving slowly, Ryan twisted until he could see his bed partner.

He swallowed as his gaze went to the back of Jeannie's head. Was it the moonlight? Jeannie's blond hair looked darker. And longer. He moved closer, took a deep breath.

"What the—" Ryan sat up so fast the whole bed shook. His hand flailed in his search for the light switch.

It wasn't Jeannie next to him. Jeannie smelled like baby powder and bananas. The woman next to him smelled exactly like…

She groaned, and as she turned over, he whispered, "No, no, no, no."

Special Agent Angie Wolf glared back at him with red-rimmed eyes.

"Jeannie is being held over in court," she snapped. "I'd rather not be here, but we don't have much choice if we want to salvage the operation."

She punched the pillow, looked once more in his direction and said, "Oh, and if you wake me before eight, I'll kill you with my bare hands," then pulled the covers over her head.

No way could Ryan pretend to be married to Angie Wolf. This operation was possible because Jeannie and he were buddies. Hell, he was pals with her husband and played with her kids.

Angie Wolf was another story. She was hot, for one thing. Hot as in smokin' hot. Tall, curvy and those legs…

God, just a few hours ago, he'd been laughing about the Intimate at Last brochure. Body work. Couples massages. *Delightful homeplay assignments.* How was this supposed to work now?

Ryan stared into the darkness. Angie Wolf was going to be his wife. For a week. Holy hell.

Pick up LYING IN BED by Jo Leigh.
On sale December 18, 2012, from Harlequin Blaze.

HBEXP1212JLREV

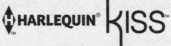